INTERFACE

Colin Andrews

www.newgeneration-publishing.com

 New Generation Publishing

Other books by Colin Andrews

Fiction:

A Matter of Degree	Matador 2011
Shattered Pretensions	Matador 2015
One Degree Over	New Generation 2018

Poems & Short Stories:

Who Gives A Hoot	New Generation 2014

Non Fiction:

Shepherd Of The Downs	Worthing Museum 1979, 1987
3rd fully revised edition	2006

www.colinandrewsauthor.co.uk

This book is dedicated to my son, Gareth Andrews

Chapter One

Sunday 27th November

I had no time to yell a warning before two men in black balaclavas grabbed my father from behind and yanked him from the chair.

The screen went blank.

I pounded my keyboard frantically trying to re-establish the Skype connection, but realised my efforts would be futile.

It had been barely ten minutes earlier that the familiar jangling tone from my laptop heralded the imminent Skype connection with my father. Within seconds his bearded face had filled my screen while my image visible to him hovered in the top right hand corner. He had leaned back, the view then exposing the top of his desk on which his left hand had rested, holding the usual glass of red wine. His face had been in shadow but light from the desk-top lamp had reflected from the thick lenses in his wire-rimmed spectacles.

"Hi, Ian, How are you doing?" His standard greeting. "Hot enough for you?"

"Going to be another scorcher, I reckon."

He may have seen the sun streaming through the window of my flat. Although only just past nine o'clock in the morning, the outside temperature was probably already pushing thirty degrees, typical of Sydney's summertime.

"Still working all God's hours?" In the short time that we had moved from emails to Skyping we had found that a Saturday evening call from my father in the UK fitted well with the one morning of the week when I was not likely to be up early for work.

"Pretty much, though things have been a bit quieter

this week." I replied casually.

"That's good. No urgent deadlines?"

"It's not quite the same as working for a daily newspaper. I've got some flexibility."

My father always seemed to bring my job into our weekly chats but I suppose it was only natural since I had no children – no wife even – for him to focus on being a granddad. I'm not sure why he'd even bothered to re-establish contact after a gap of over twenty years. Loneliness perhaps; he'd told me that his second wife, in a childless marriage, had passed away recently, or maybe he was trying belatedly to make amends after walking out on my mother when I was just four years old. I had received a birthday card from him every year until I was sixteen but he hadn't even bothered to get in touch when Mum died three years ago.

I admit I'd been a bit wary when I received an email from him out of the blue less than six weeks ago but I didn't really feel any animosity towards him. My mother had been quite philosophical about the divorce and had not poisoned my mind.

Even so, our conversations were rather stilted as we had little obviously in common apart from our genes. Relaxed informality between father and son was still a long way off. He'd asked whether I had any plans to return to the UK. I'd told him I hadn't. Then.

I'd noticed some movement in the shadows behind my father's chair. Too late.

For a moment I sat there, almost frozen, as my mind couldn't believe what my eyes had just seen.

I picked up my phone to call the police but then realised that it would be pointless. Sydney police wouldn't be in the least interested in a possible abduction the other side of the world.

I Googled the Metropolitan Police hoping to find some international number I could use. Bingo!

"I wish to report an assault," I began.

"Sir, may I ask where you are calling from?"

"I'm in Sydney but ..."

"If the alleged assault was there I'm afraid we cannot help you."

"Not, it was in London. My father lives there. We were talking on Skype when two men grabbed him and I lost contact."

"When did this happen?"

"Just a few minutes ago."

"Do you have your father's address – and his name, of course?"

"It's John Fielder." I realised that he'd not yet given me his full postal address. "He lives in Lewisham."

"I will need you to be more specific, sir."

I racked my brains. I'm pretty sure I hadn't written down anything but I was sure he'd mentioned something else. Station? No, railway! "I think it's Railway Road or Lane, or something like that." I thought I had heard the odd rattle of trains in the background on some occasions.

The operator seemed surprised that I didn't have my father's address but I explained that we had only re-established contact recently after a long gap. "Station Road, Lewisham or Railway Terrace, perhaps? There's a Railway Terrace in Ladywell, which is near Lewisham High Street," she replied, after a few seconds clacking away on her keyboard.

"Railway Terrace, most likely." It rang a bell in my mind.

"And your name, sir?"

"Ian Fielder." I gave her my current address, email and mobile phone.

"Thank you. We will look into the matter and get back to you. It may be tomorrow morning, though."

I wasn't hopeful of a positive outcome. Without a specific address and an informant thousands of miles away I very much doubted it would be given high priority. I could have even been a hoax caller.

3

Chapter 2

Monday 28th November

As I sat in the departure lounge of Kingsford Smith, Sydney's airport, I couldn't get my father's image out of my mind. Although I'd only known him for a few short weeks I felt some kind of responsibility for him. Irrationally, I suppose.

I'd made up my mind even before the Metropolitan Police rang back late on Sunday evening. I knew that I had not been hallucinating and I needed to know what had really happened. I wasn't going to get the answer sitting on my backside in Sydney. The London police had been quite apologetic but had reported that no-one by the name of John Fielder was known to the residents of Railway Terrace and no-one had seen or heard any suspicious activity at the time of the alleged assault.

I'd rung Howard, my editor, first thing on Monday morning to ask for a week's leave 'on urgent family business'. Since I'd joined the company a couple of years ago he'd been very supportive. He gave me pretty much a free rein in my investigations, with the occasional suggestion as to where to focus if I seemed to be going up a blind alley. He'd agreed to my request since there had been very little recent activity from the activists in Australia that were the subject of my current investigations, and the copy date for the proposed major article was still nearly two months away. He'd also offered to make the booking since the company enjoyed some good discounts with several major carriers. Unsurprisingly, he wasn't so taken with my suggestion of claiming expenses for the trip in order to do a comparison with similar groups in the UK. The ticket had arrived by email within a few minutes, with a note to say he would deduct the cost from my salary!

The mid-afternoon flight to Singapore was not fully booked. I had the choice of the three seats between aisle and window. Five hours of high altitude viewing of the Australian outback had little appeal and I used the journey to plan the best use of my visit in London. And to check on the location of places I might need to visit.

Conversely, there were few, if any, spare seats on the long haul from Changi Airport to Heathrow. I'd barely settled down in my allocated aisle seat when I had to move for an overweight elderly Asian woman to squeeze past into the window seat. A couple of minutes later a young woman, smartly but casually dressed, approached, anxiously scanning the seat numbers displayed by the luggage lockers. She stopped by my seat.

"Fifty-two? Row fifty- two?" She asked, flicking back her long brunette hair. Lovely soft voice.

I nodded, and stood to let her take her place beside me, once she had stowed away her small travel bag in the overhead locker.

"Thank you very much,"

Very soon the Airbus began to ease away from the terminal and taxi to the runway. With the vast expanse of Changi Airport one seemed to be travelling miles even before take-off.

My new companion peered through the plane's window.

"I'm afraid you won't see much of Singapore," I said, "only the lights, much the same view as any large international airport."

"Oh, what a pity." She turned back to me. "This is my first trip outside Australia."

"Were you on the flight from Sydney? I didn't see you."

"No, I came up from Melbourne. Only had an hour or so at Singapore." She fidgeted to get comfortable in the seat, restrained by the seat belt. "Are you on holiday?"

"Not really," I said, "A family visit." To my father if I can find him, I thought. I hadn't got any other relatives in the UK, at least that I was aware of.

"That's why you've got a British accent then!"

"I guess so, though it's probably the only connection I've now got to the UK "

"Apart from your father."

"Uh huh," hopefully. "And yourself? Holiday?"

"A school friend moved to London last year, and she invited me to come and stay. She's a nurse."

We braced ourselves for take-off. The girl looked tense, and gripped the armrests tightly until the seatbelt signs were switched off.

She took a couple of deep breaths. "Silly I know, but take-off always scares me."

The cabin crew came round with hot moist towels prior to serving dinner – or whatever they called it at midnight local time.

"Do you know London well?" She asked.

"Not really, I'm from the West of England originally but I worked in Shepherd's Bush for a couple of years."

"Is that anywhere near Lewisham?"

I shook my head. I didn't want to pursue that particular topic. Further conversation concerning our destination was curtailed anyway by the stewards collecting the used towels, followed very soon after by the serving of a three course meal and coffee. Surprisingly tasty for pre-packed airline food.

I was also pleasantly surprised by how quickly I must have fallen asleep once the cabin lights had been turned down. Apart from an occasional vague awareness of some people brushing past me along the aisle, it was some six hours later that I was fully conscious again. And became aware of the young woman's head resting peacefully on my shoulder.

I let her remain undisturbed until my bladder took priority. I gently eased myself from the seat.

She woke with a start and probably realised that she'd been using my shoulder as a pillow. She was effusively apologetic when I returned to my seat.

"It's okay," I said, "But perhaps you could introduce yourself. It's not every day I wake up with an attractive young woman by my side."

She blushed.

"I'm sorry," I said, "That was a bit forward of me."

"No, no. No offence taken. I'm Amy, Amy Cadwallader."

"Ian Fielder. Your name sounds Cornish."

"Perhaps. I think my great-grandfather was a miner."

"Are you spending all the time with your friend?"

"Two or three weeks in all but I may take a few days doing the tourist thing. What about yourself?"

"Short visit, I expect. I'm supposed to be back at work next week."

"And what kind of work is that?"

"I'm a writer." I thought that sounded more appealing than journalist.

"Really? Fiction?"

"No, mostly features for magazines," I said. I didn't really want to go into details of my investigative work. "What about you? Are you a nurse like your friend?"

"No, I work in a library."

We chatted informally through the serving of breakfast and until the plane began its descent to Heathrow. Amy once again grew tense and gripped her seat, and didn't relax until we were taxiing towards the terminal.

All in all, it had been a pleasant flight and I wished her well as we prepared for disembarkation. I didn't expect to see her again.

I was wrong.

Chapter 3

Tuesday 29th November

My budget limited the accommodation I could afford even for a short stay. The Dorchester was definitely off-limits so I'd found on-line an inexpensive small hotel in Kensington. I preferred to be in a part of the city with which I had some familiarity rather than the eastern suburbs that were foreign territory. I probably knew the suburbs of Sydney better.

My next priority after checking in was to head over to Lewisham, though I was not optimistic about what I'd find. My in-flight internet search had shown that Lewisham was at the terminus of the Dockland Light Railway but the best option for me seemed to be the overground from Victoria. I purchased an A-Z street map along with an Oyster card.

Alighting at Lewisham station, the adjacent Station Road seemed a logical place to start searching for my father's abode. My initial impression was that it would be an easy task as it obviously wasn't a residential area and there were no terraced cottages. Two huge apartment blocks quickly dispelled that myth – River Mill and Fizzy Lewisham Brick Kiln. I'd seen the latter on-line and assumed it was probably a craft brewery.

I very much doubted whether the police had checked all the residents as a result of my phone call.

They were my next port of call.

The officer behind the reception desk could have come straight out of a vintage TV drama – big, burly, receding hairline and a walrus moustache. But he was friendly in his attitude.

"How can I help you, sir?"

I explained what I'd seen on Skype and recounted my conversations with the met.

"And you've come all this way?" he said, in astonishment.

"Well, he is my father and I would really like to find out what has happened to him."

"Yes, I understand. Saturday evening you say?"

"Saturday evening here, Sunday morning back home."

"Give me a moment, and I'll check."

He disappeared behind a glazed partition. I could see him talking with a colleague.

"Right," he said, a couple of minutes later. "A patrol car did visit Railway Terrace at Ladywell – that's just down the road from here – on Saturday evening, and an officer spoke to those residents who were at home. No-one reported anything amiss, and no-one it seems had heard of a John Fielder."

The same response I'd already received by telephone.

"Are you sure you had the right address?" the officer asked.

"Not absolutely," I admitted. "I hadn't ever written it down." I didn't mention that to my recollection my father had never given me his full address. "Did you check Station Road?" I said hopefully.

"No, I'm sorry. We weren't asked to. I'm sorry we haven't been able to find out what happened to your father."

"Okay, but thanks anyway. You've done as much as you could, given the rather vague information."

"What are you planning to do now? Return to Australia?"

"Not yet. I'll talk with letting agents to see if my father rented somewhere. Perhaps check the electoral roll. And I'll just take a look at Railway Terrace. There may be someone at home who wasn't around on Saturday evening."

"Well, good luck, sir. And take care."

I lost count of how many Estate Agents I visited that afternoon. Several along Lewisham's High Street alone. A few were very helpful, the others very wary, even when I showed them my passport as proof of identity to establish my connection with a possible tenant. One obliging, matronly receptionist asked I had a photo of my father as she claimed she had a good memory for faces. The only images I had of him were on Skype – and a screen shot was the last thing on my mind before we were cut off.

All my enquiries were to no avail. No-one had a John Fielder on their books as tenant, landlord or house buyer in Lewisham or in the neighbouring areas that were covered by any particular agency. Unless, perchance, he had rented or purchased under a different name, though why he would do that I couldn't imagine.

I reckoned I had just enough time to check the electoral role at the Council offices.

My disappointment at again drawing a blank must have been obvious to the clerk who had helped me.

"You are aware that people can request their name to be removed from the open register available to the public?"

Bugger! "No I wasn't, but thanks for telling me." Wherever my father was living he seemed to be keeping the details well hidden.

In late November, it was already getting dark by the time I left the council offices. As I made my way back to the High Street I had to make up my mind as to my next priority; to visit Railway Terrace or to get something to eat. Perhaps more residents would be home if I left the door-to-door job until a little later. A snazzy pub, the Fox and Firkin, caught my eye and my dilemma was resolved.

God, I needed that pint!

Railway Terrace was a quiet cul-de-sac with a few quite modern residential properties facing, unsurprisingly, the railway line and Ladywell station. Three youths were leaning against the railings, smoking and swigging beer from cans.

I knocked at each door and explained to those who were reluctant to remove the security chain from their door that I was not selling, preaching or canvassing but trying to find my father whom I believed lived in this street.

"Never heard of him," or "Police already asked that question." were the usual responses. One old lady, who apparently hadn't been home when the police called, knitted her already well-wrinkled brow, "Fielder, you say? Sure it wasn't Bowler? We had a nice young man next door called Bowler." She obviously detected some surprise from me at the sporting connection. "My late husband was a keen cricketer. Used to play until his knees gave out – and then he'd be glued to the telly for all the test matches."

I thanked her. I held back from commenting that I really was certain of my own father's surname. Anyway, young wouldn't have described my father.

The next house – the end of the row – where Mr Bowler had lived was empty. It looked as if it had been so for some time, and the 'For Sale' sign definitely looked as if it had taken root in the ground. On an impulse I crossed the grassed area to look at the rear. One window had been boarded up on the inside to cover the broken pane, quite recently judging by the condition of the wood.

I was beginning to feel the effects of my long day, not to mention the long flight. Not that I felt any effect of jet lag as such. Having the station so close by was a bonus. Darkness had now fallen and most of the street lights were working

The youths were still lounging in the same place. As I entered the station I noticed the tallest one, a swarthy youth with a shaved head, throw his dog end and can in the gutter and move in my direction.

The platform was almost deserted. A train rattled in – only four carriages, and very few passengers. As I stepped aboard the three youths sprinted from the station entrance and pushed in around me.

"Excuse me," I said politely and much more calmly than I felt as the train started to move, "I would like to sit down." There was only one other occupant of the carriage – an old bloke reading a newspaper.

"Not gonna happen, mate," Shaven-head sneered.

"You want my money?" I reached for the wallet in my back pocket.

"Nah."

The old bloke was beginning to notice that something was amiss. Another of the trio, a beer-bellied bearded guy with tattoos on his neck, turned to him, and waggled his index finger, then drew it across his neck in a cut-throat gesture. The old guy quickly buried his head in his paper.

Three to one wasn't good odds but I'd always been told that attack was the best form of defence. I kneed Shaven-head in the bollocks and then hacked back with my heel onto Beer-gut's shin. Both roared in pain but the third guy drew a knife, pulled me around and lunged at my chest. I staggered and fell. My last memory was of the train slowing down for the next station as my head exploded in pain from a heavy blow.

Chapter 4

Wednesday 30th November

My head felt like a hundred demons were hammering to get out of my skull. I tried to lever myself up and winced as a shaft of pain seared through my left side. Groggily I struggled to open my eyes.

"Take it easy, Ian, you've been injured."

Ian? Who knew me in London? Yet the voice was familiar. My eyes focussed.

"Amy? What ... ? Where am I?"

"You're in Lewisham Hospital. You were attacked on a train by some hooligans who ran off and left you bleeding."

I recalled the confrontation. "But ... why are you here?"

"My friend, the nurse, I'm staying with was on duty when they brought you in last night. She mentioned it to me this morning. I wanted to see that you were okay."

"Thank ... er ... thank you! I really appreciate your kind thoughts. Though we don't really know each other."

"Well we did sleep together – in a manner of speaking."

My turn to blush, beneath the bandage round my head. Something puzzled me, though. "How did you know it was me in the hospital? Did your friend actually mention my name?"

"Er, no. She looked pretty tired at breakfast and I asked her if she'd had a busy night. She said that this young man had been nearly killed. A blood-stained business card found in his shirt pocket showed he was an Australian journalist. I asked her to describe him, and told her that it was probably the person I'd sat next to on the flight. I was very worried."

A nurse approached my bed and spoke to Amy.

"I'll have to go now, I'm afraid. The doctor and the police want to talk to you," she said.

"Will you be back?"

"If you want me to."

"I'd really like that."

"Okay but I'm not sure how long they intend to keep you here."

A thought came to me. "Amy, could you do something for me?"

"Yes of course."

"Please contact my hotel in Kensington – the St Marks – and let them know that I'm … I've been in an accident … but to keep my room."

"Okay." She even blew me a kiss.

The nurse pulled the curtains round my bed and a young doctor of Indian ethnicity entered. His name badge identified him as Dr. N. Patel.

"Good morning, Mr. Fielder. How are you feeling?"

"I've felt better."

"You are quite fortunate to be able to say so. You were stabbed in the chest but the blade struck your mobile phone and was deflected to give just a superficial flesh wound. Otherwise you would now be lying in the mortuary. You also had a nasty bump on the head. Someone put the boot in, I'd guess."

"How long will I be in hospital?"

"We've kept you in for observation – possible concussion, you understand. But all being well you can go home this afternoon. You'll need to change the dressing but you can get that done nearer home if more convenient. We will give you our phone number if you need to make an appointment here." He paused, "Where do you live?"

"In Sydney. I'm visiting – staying in a hotel."

"Ah, I see. And your girlfriend?"

"She's not actually my girlfriend. We happened to be sitting next to each other on the flight from Singapore. She is staying with a nurse who works in this hospital."

"Well perhaps we can suggest she keeps an eye on you for a while."

I was beginning to feel a bit dozy again after he left. I had about ten minutes respite before the police arrived. A middle-aged woman with long dark hair was obviously in charge. Curves in all the right places but already showing an inclination to spread out. Her companion was a beanpole of a bloke with sandy hair.

"Good morning. I'm Detective Inspector Jayne Myers and my colleague is DC Parsons. Do you feel fit enough to answer a few questions?"

"I'll try."

"Okay, now we are treating this assault as attempted murder, since the doctors inform us that the stabbing could have been fatal. We know that three young men were seen running from the station at Lewisham. You were found unconscious and bleeding by the door of the train," the inspector said.

"The three youths crowded me onto the train at Ladywell, and immediately began to intimidate me. I was pretty sure they were going to beat me up so I struggled and one of them drew a knife. Next thing I know I'm here in hospital."

"Had you seen them before?" The DC this time.

"They were outside the station earlier."

"Doing what?"

"Nothing, except smoking and drinking."

"And what were you doing?" asked Inspector Myers.

"Calling at houses."

"For what reason?"

"I'm trying to find where my father lived."

The penny must have dropped with the young detective. "You were in the police station yesterday, I believe."

"That's right."

He had a word on the side with his superior. She nodded, then addressed me again.

"Can you describe your attackers?"

"One was tall, well-built, with a shaven head. Grey bomber jacket and jeans. Another was shorter, fatter and bearded. He'd got an eagle – a double-headed eagle tattooed on his neck. The third one – I didn't get a good look at him. Thinner, average height, weasely face and a couple of piercings in each ear."

The two detectives looked at each other.

"You know them?" I asked.

"They were white?" asked the inspector.

"Yes."

"They are known to the police," said DI Myers. "Strange, picking on you, though. They usually target blacks and Asians, with threatening behaviour and intimidation, though rarely any physical violence – unless their victim retaliates. They make no secret of their support for the English Defence League."

"We have some cretins like that down under, in Australia."

The inspector thought for a moment. "Tell me, do you think there could be any connection between the assault you reported on your father and the assault on you?"

"I can't imagine why there should be. I haven't really known him all that long. I don't know what he was into, don't know anything about his profession, or even if he was still working. I had assumed he was retired."

She grimaced, "Okay for now. Let me have a phone number where I can contact you, if necessary, and I'd also appreciate knowing in advance when you intend to return to Australia. If you do think of anything else that might be relevant please get in touch."

When the police had left I reflected on the questions

the inspector had raised. Could there be a connection between my father's abduction and the attempt on my life? If I had not made the first move I might not have been stabbed, but I certainly had had the feeling that they had intended to inflict some damage to my person. Perhaps my father's attackers thought that he might have passed some crucial information on to me – though Christ knows what that might have been? And how would those youths have known where to find me? I'd told the police of course – and practically all the estate agents in Lewisham were aware that I was looking for a John Fielder possibly in Railway Terraces. But there seemed to be no evidence that he had actually lived there. I needed to find out a lot more about my father.

I must have slept for a couple of hours. When I awoke lunch was being served in the ward.

The nurse I'd seen earlier came over to me. "Mr. Fielder, subject to a final check by Dr. Patel you will be able to leave hospital later this afternoon. It might be better if you got a taxi rather than public transport."

"Thanks, I will."

*****

Amy insisted on seeing me safely back to my hotel and I only put up a token objection. In truth, I was glad of her company.

"Did you get to see your father before your, er, mishap," she asked when we had settled into the taxi.

"No, I'm afraid I didn't."

"Does he live in Lewisham? I was quite surprised when I heard you'd been found at the station there."

"Well, I thought he did."

"Sorry, I don't understand."

"That makes two of us," I took a deep breath – or as deep as my knife wound would allow. "It's complicated."

"Do you want to tell me?"

I felt the need to share my thoughts and perhaps get an unbiased view. "Long or short version?"

"As you wish."

I opted for a slightly edited version. I didn't need to burden her with all my family background.

"That's really weird," she said when I had finished. "What are you going to do now?"

"Now," I said, "I'm going to ask you to have dinner with me. You've been a tremendous support even though we barely know each other."

"You don't have to ..."

"Please, it's the least I can do."

Chapter 5

Thursday 1st December

I woke up with a sore head. Not this time because of contact with a hard object but due to the quantity of wine I'd consumed with our dinner. I'd insisted on paying for Amy to get a taxi back to her friend's house, after we'd walked the short distance from the restaurant to my hotel. We had agreed to meet again while we were still both in London though we left the details rather fluid as I wasn't at all sure where my investigations into my father would take me next.

My room phone rang just as I was about to head down for a late breakfast.

"Mr Fielder? There are two police officers here in reception who would like to have a word with you."

Perhaps they now had some news about my father. "Okay, I'll be there directly."

They weren't either of the officers who had interviewed me in hospital. Both were heavily built, possibly both former rugby forwards. One had a broken nose. He looked the more senior of the two. Definitely older. He spoke first.

"Good morning, Mr Fielder. We'd like to ask you some more questions."

"You have some more information about my father?" I said hopefully.

A brief nod but no direct answer. "If you would accompany us to the police station we can sort it out there."

"Is that really necessary?" I replied, "I'm quite happy to sort it out here."

"I must insist …"

I couldn't see why I would need to go to the police station. Mortuary, perhaps, if they had found my father's body. "You can insist all you like but unless you are arresting me I have no intention of accompanying you to the police station at the moment. Later perhaps." I said firmly.

"Very well, if that's the way you want it ..."

I cut him off again. "That's ridiculous!" I was getting pissed off with his attitude. I had another thought – or rather suspicion. "By the way, you haven't introduced yourself yet. I want to see your warrant cards."

The younger one glanced at his boss, and spoke for the first time, "We've left them in the car."

Like hell. "Okay you go and get your warrant cards, and I'll get my coat from my room."

Broken nose made a move to put his hand on my shoulder. I brushed it off and called over to the receptionist whom I noticed had been watching our exchanges. "Did you check these gentlemen really were police officers?"

Quickly I took the stairs back to my first floor room. I took the card I'd been given by DI Myers at the hospital and called the number on my mobile. I was pleased that my phone was still working, after having taken the blow from the knife.

Fortunately she answered personally. I asked her if she knew of any reason why a couple of other police officers were asking me to go with them to the police station.

"We have no need to question you further, Mr Fielder, though we will need you to make a formal statement if we are to press charges against those youths who assaulted you. We haven't been able to track them down yet. Tell me, what names did these officers give?"

"They didn't. And they claimed they had left their warrant cards in the car."

"That just would not happen! Are they still there at

your hotel?"

"I don't know but I very much doubt it. I told them to have their cards when I returned from my room with my coat."

She asked for descriptions, which I provided as best I could. "They don't match with any serving officer at this station."

When I went back down, there was no sign of the heavies in reception.

I was desperate for a coffee. Over breakfast, I mulled over the incident. I was pretty certain that I would not have been taken to a police station for questioning, nor would any interrogation have been undertaken within legal guidelines. Not that I knew a darn thing about my father's predicament other than what I had witnessed briefly on the screen.

The questions also came to my mind not only of who wanted to get hold of me, but why – and also how they knew where to find me. Lewisham police only had my mobile number. While my intention to visit Railway Terrace had been shared with a number of people, only Amy knew where I was staying in London. I didn't recall leaving any forwarding address at the hospital. I suppose it was possible that we had been followed though it seemed unlikely.

Could Amy have been a plant? From what I'd seen of her so far she would have had to have been an extremely good actress. And she would have to have been briefed somehow before she left Australia by someone who knew I was going to London to find out what had happened to my father. Whilst I had planned to ring her later in the day, I wasn't sure that I could trust her without doing some checking on the details of her personal background that she had revealed over last night's dinner.

There were a hell of a lot of other things that needed to be checked, and I didn't have the time or resources, or perhaps even the know-how to do what was necessary.

When I'd worked in London I'd shared a flat in Barnes with a young geek called Dominic whose whole life seemed to revolve around computers. His day job was with some software development company though he'd often work from home. Apart from the odd shared mealtime and a pint with me in a pub he seemed to spend most of his time in his room in front of a screen. I suspected that some of his activities were of dubious legality. We'd kept in touch for a couple of years after I moved to Sydney but only an occasional email since.

He responded to my email almost immediately and invited me to call round later that morning.

Apart from seeking his help in doing some internet searches for me, I had another major request to make of him. I felt it was unwise to stay at my hotel any longer as my presence there was obviously known to the 'opposition' – whoever they were. It was quite possible they were still watching the hotel but I took the opportunity of leaving with a small group who were heading for Earl's Court. The tube could have taken me to Heathrow but I hopped off at Hammersmith just as the doors were closing, then quickly made my way up to the bus station for the short ride to Barnes.

Dom hadn't changed since I'd last seen him. Long hair crudely held back with a rubber band in a ponytail. A thin, pointed beard which accentuated his already long, thin face. Thick horn-rimmed glasses completed the nerdy image.

"Good to see you mate!" His welcome seemed very genuine. "But what's all this cloak and dagger stuff with finding somewhere to kip? You haven't got a woman chasing after you?"

A possibility, I thought. When I'd checked my mobile before leaving the hotel there had been three missed calls and a couple of texts from Amy. I'd switched it off in case someone was checking my movements. I'd bought a cheap pay-as-you go – an untraceable burner for any necessary calls while I was in the UK.

"Anyway, Ian," Dom continued, "You're lucky that the bloke who took your place here has just moved on and I haven't got a replacement yet."

Over a coffee, we got down to business, and I gave him a brief summary of why I was back in the UK and why I was seeking his help.

"So let's be clear," he said, "you want me to run a background check on a young woman from Melbourne and find the current address of a John Fielder, possibly in Lewisham. Anything else?"

"Yes, that's about it – for starters."

"Bloody hell – and you want this when?"

"By yesterday, ideally. But as soon as you can. I'm supposed to be back at work next week."

"Doing what? A reporter for whatever is the Oz equivalent of the BBC?"

"No, I'm an investigative journalist for a magazine."

"Investigating what?"

"My last assignment was on child pornography. A couple of CEOs and a junior minister resigned their posts in exchange for their names not appearing in my article. I didn't make any promises about what information I would pass on to the police, though."

"And what's your latest mission?"

I hesitated. I tended to keep the topic of any current investigation pretty close to my chest. But Dom wouldn't have shown any reaction if I'd claimed to be on a mission to blow up Buckingham Palace. The new focus for my efforts had been triggered by the racist attack on a neighbouring family with whom I was quite friendly. My progress so far had been fairly limited, short on names and lacking specific evidence. However, I had already discovered enough information to be pretty certain that, beyond the street corner yobbos looking for any excuse for aggro and beyond the very public face of loud-mouthed fringe politicians, there was a well-organised but well-concealed network of extremists.

"I'm looking at the rise of the far-right in Australia."

"Nazis, you mean?"

"Yes, sort of."

"Well we've got some right basket cases over here. They are none too happy about our new prime minister, him being black and gay."

"Yes, I did see some crude graffiti on a tunnel wall on my way here."

"And what are you planning to do while I'm chasing your father and girl friend?"

"She's not...." I began then saw that Dom was taking the piss. "I'm going to see if I can find out anything about my father's employment."

Dom raised his eyebrows, "How?"

"I think he was some kind of civil servant, according to my mother. Mind you, that's a long time ago."

"Well, I suggest you try the National Archives at Kew. You may be lucky."

"Yes, I will, thanks." Just a short train journey from Barnes Bridge. "How about we meet up later at that real ale pub we used to go to? I'll buy you a pint."

"Is that all my efforts are worth?" Dom tried to look pained.

"Okay, at least two pints. And a take away pizza."

*****

The staff at the National Archives were helpful, as far as was possible, given the limited information that I had to go on. If it was like looking for a needle in a haystack I hoped I at least had the right haystack!

I found not one but three needles. Three persons by

the name of John Fielder who had at some point been employed by Her Majesty's Government. One who had been a senior advisor to the defence secretary between the wars I rejected immediately. He would have been old enough to be my grandfather. Another was listed as being an attaché in the Diplomatic Service while the third held some unspecified post in the Civil Service.

Dom's glass was already nearly due for a refill by the time I got to the Bricklayer's Arms in Putney. We'd visited the popular real ale pub a few times when I'd shared the flat with him, as it was an easy walk from the station. On one occasion in the summer we had even walked along the banks of the Thames from Barnes.

"Same again?" I asked. He nodded, and I ordered two pints of Timothy Taylor's Landlord, which had found an appreciative market far from its Yorkshire roots.

"Any joy?" I said when we'd settled down at a table at the back of the bar.

"Well, you certainly set me a challenge."

"And?" My impatience was difficult to restrain.

"Your fair lass … she seems genuine enough. Born and raised in Melbourne, parents still around, I think. One brother, a couple of years older. Apart from the nurse friend you mentioned I can't find any other connection with London, or for that matter, with Sydney. Oh and by the way, she's single and not in a relationship with anybody, as far as I can tell."

I was amazed, "How did you find all that out?"

He touched a finger to his nose, "Best you don't know."

I felt somewhat relieved that she probably hadn't directed the fake plods to my hotel.

Dom took a couple of generous swigs and continued, "Your father – not so straightforward. I've found no record of any John Fielder living in Lewisham, and that's going back a decade with the electoral roll and national census. But there's more than a bus load of them in Greater

London, let alone the rest of the country, and without some way of narrowing it down I'm not sure what further progress I can make." He shrugged his shoulders, "Sorry. Anyway, how did you get on?"

"A couple of possibles from government employment records," I replied, and gave him a brief account of what I'd found.

"Hmm, that may help," he said, without much confidence. "It would be good if you had a birth date, or at least some definite indication of his age.

I had a thought. "Births, marriages and deaths," I said. "There should be a record of his marriage to my mother. I know her maiden name, and where they got married. His details should be there. And possibly divorce papers? He told me he'd married again so there should be another record somewhere."

"Yeah, I can work on that. Now how about that pizza?"

As we headed off for the main street and its choice of eateries I switched on my mobile. More missed calls and texts from Amy all with the same urgent message, "Ring me – please!" Still wary about possible remote tracking, I noted her number, switched off my smartphone and called her on the pre-paid set.

"Hello?" She sounded nervous.

"Amy? This is Ian."

"Ian! Oh thank God! Are you okay?"

"Yes, I'm alright, "I said guardedly, "Why..."

"I've been trying to contact you, and when you didn't answer I was so scared that I might have put you in danger."

"What do you mean?"

"Two horrible blokes came banging on my friend's door early this morning. Cassie wasn't back from her shift. She'd been called into work. They threatened to take me down the police station if I didn't tell them your address."

Chapter 6

Friday 2nd December : morning

I set out early. My journey was quite long, though relatively straightforward by train with only a couple of changes to Forest Hill. Even though I still had a walk uphill from the station I thought it unlikely that anyone would have tracked me from Dom's pad.

I was more worried about Amy since she would probably still be seen by my unknown opponents as the best link to me. She'd become quite agitated when I'd told her that her unwelcome visitors had indeed called on me, but I had reassured her that I'd called the bluff of the fake cops. I explained that as a precaution I'd kept my smart phone switched off and also checked out of the hotel. However when I'd suggested that it would be in her own interests to avoid any further contact with me in London and just enjoy the stay with her friend, she had been most insistent that she wanted to see me, one more time, at least.

I'd been hesitant in arranging anything formal but she had persuaded me to meet up with her on a sightseeing trip that Cassie had planned for that morning when she was not working. The cold and windy weather had been largely responsible for the choice of venue.

I was pretty sure that a bus from Lewisham would drop Cassie and Amy close to the entrance of the Horniman Museum. My early arrival gave me the advantage of looking out for anyone obviously following them.

No-one appeared to take any interest in them when they alighted from the bus, but as it began to pull away a grey saloon pulled in behind it. A passenger quickly got out and focussed his gaze on Amy and Cassie who were slowly walking up to the museum entrance. I recognised him as the younger of my two hotel visitors. He made no move to follow but scanned the street, presumably looking for some sign of my presence.

I withdrew into the lobby of the Museum and dialled 999.

Amy and Cassie didn't appear inside until a few minutes after I'd heard the sound of police sirens.

They passed through into the main body of the museum. I waited to check that they were no longer being followed. I caught up with them just as they had entered a gallery apparently dedicated to musical instruments.

"Ian! You're here!" Amy gave me a hug, "I'm so pleased to see you." She pulled back. "Here, you haven't met Cassie yet.""

Cassie stood a good head above Amy but slightly shorter than me, about five foot nine I'd guess. She was slender with blue eyes and long blond hair. Quite a stunning figure but overall rather spoiled by a rather large, beaky nose and puffy cheeks. It wasn't improved by her smile which made her look like a predatory carnivore. Friendly enough manner, though. "Good to see you looking much better than when they brought you into A & E."

"Hi, Cassie. Yes Thanks to you and your colleagues I'm still here to tell the tale."

"And a pretty strange tale, from what Amy's told me."

"Indeed. And it's on-going. Did you hear the sirens outside?"

"Yes, Amy and I heard them. Just as a police car was pulling up behind this car at the bus stop a bloke suddenly dived onto the back seat and it pulled out straight into the stream of traffic. It roared away, with the police in pursuit."

"I think they were the men that threatened Amy at your house yesterday morning then tried to take me from my hotel."

"What!" Amy's hand flew to her mouth.

"I saw the car. The bloke who got out was looking at you. I recognised him from yesterday morning. I called the police and said that you were in danger of being attacked by a stalker."

"That's scary!"

Cassie frowned. Perhaps Amy hadn't told her about yesterday's early morning call.

"Shall we sit down and have a coffee? I don't think we are going to be troubled by that pair again today but there are some things we need to talk about." I suggested.

We gathered our drinks and some slices of flapjack and settled down at a table where I could keep an eye on the entrance – just in case.

"Amy, I began, "I don't know what's happening but I really don't want to put you in any more danger by getting involved in my problems."

She shrugged, "It's ok ..."

"No, really, you implied on the plane that you were going to spend some your time sightseeing in this country. I think now would be a good time to do that."

"What about you?" she asked.

"Well, I've still got some possible leads to follow up. Though I haven't had much joy so far."

Amy looked at Cassie. "What do you think? Would you be able to come with me?"

Cassie thought for a few moments before replying. "Tricky," she said. "I've been called in to cover for a couple more nights but then I'm free after the weekend. Until then I can only fit in local visits like this. Sorry about that, Amy, I expected to be free when I invited you to visit. What Ian is suggesting makes sense. I'm quite happy to recommend some places and sort out accommodation, if you like."

"That would be very helpful," Amy said.

She started to say something to me but held back. She looked as if she was not entirely happy with the prospect of being a solo tourist. She may even have been disappointed that we were unlikely to see each other again in the UK.

I fished a business card out of my pocket, "I hope we can meet up sometime when we're both back home, in more, um, normal circumstances. Do please get in touch."

"Thank you, Ian, I'd like that."

"By the way, Ian, when are you intending to return to Australia?" Cassie asked.

"I'm supposed to be back at work by Wednesday so I'd have to leave very early Tuesday at the latest."

"So where are your staying till then?"

"With an old friend."

There didn't seem much point in lingering around. Though the museum looked very interesting, I had more pressing matters to attend to, so I left them to enjoy the rest of the day unhindered by my problems.

My phone trilled as I was walking back to the station.

"Hi, Ian, it's Dom." He sounded excited, "You'll never believe this! It seems your father died about two months ago."

Chapter 7

Friday 2nd December : afternoon

During my journey back to Barnes I tried to make some sense of the situation. While I hadn't expected on my trip to London to necessarily discover exactly what had happened to my father, I had anticipated finding that he had at least been very recently alive and at an easily traceable address. Perversely, at every stage I had been presented with yet more unanswered questions. If my father had already died more than a month before he had supposedly made contact with me, then who was masquerading as my father? And why? How had this person found my details? And why should he then have been attacked in front of my eyes?

One thing was certain. If I were to have any hope of finding an answer to any of these questions I would have to postpone my return to Sydney. It was now Friday. Public offices would be closed over the weekend. I couldn't honestly see any hope of resolution in the single working day remaining before my intended flight from Heathrow.

It would already be late evening in Sydney but I sent a text to my boss advising him that I needed a few more days. He might not be happy but I'd sort out the consequences later.

Dom met me at the Waterman's Arms, which had been more or less our local when we hadn't wanted to make the trip to Putney. It had a good range of real ales and good food.

"That was a bombshell," I said. "Did you find an address?"

"Well, sort of. Nothing in Lewisham if that's what you

were thinking. It was a private hotel in Camden Town."

"Christ almighty." I took a deep breath. "Probably completely pointless going there now."

"Another dead end?" said Dom, grinning.

"Very funny. Tell me, did you find out how he died?"

"Yeah, that's a bit odd too. Hit and run accident. They never did find the driver."

I was beginning to think that my father might have got involved in some dodgy activity or perhaps had some information for which public disclosure would have been unwelcome to some group or individual. Perhaps a colleague had taken up my father's discoveries, and for some reason wanted to pass them on to me. And whoever had been responsible for my father's death had also taken out his colleague, and sought to do the same with me in case I'd been given this damaging data.

All speculation of course. Truth is, I still hadn't got a clue as to what had really happened or why.

"Did you find out anything else?" I said, resigned to yet another disappointment.

"As a matter of fact I did. He had an elder brother, Peter. Your uncle, I suppose."

"But is he still alive?"

"Seems so."

"Any chance of an address?"

"He's on the South coast. Place called Arundel. Do you know it?"

"I've heard of it. Somewhere in Sussex I think. I've never been there, though."

"Mind you I don't know how recent the address is."

With a name and address I might be lucky enough to find a phone number. Unlike my generation for whom a mobile was the prime telephone service, an older chap was more likely to still rely on a landline.

"Same again?" I said, as Dom drained his pint.

He nodded.

When I returned from the bar with two pints of Big Smoke Solaris, a brew I'd never heard of before, and a couple of bags of crisps, Dom looked deep in thought.

"What are you planning to do next, Ian? Is there anything else you need me to do? I've been rather neglecting the jobs that bring in the money chasing after your lost relatives."

"I'm sorry, Dom, I do really appreciate what you've done." I took a swig. "Very gluggable, this." Then to business. "First priority now, I think, is to try to contact this Uncle Peter, and if possible meet up with him. I need to find out who was posing as my father and why. I'd like to discover what line of work my father was in. I don't suppose you've had any joy there?"

"Not really. From the leads you gave me from Kew I think it very likely that he was in public or government service. I can dig a bit deeper, if you like."

"That would be helpful. And also, any details about his fatal accident."

Dom rolled his eyes, "Okay. Are you coming back to the flat tonight?"

"Depends. Let's head back there now. I need to make some phone calls."

We picked up a couple of pasties from a bakery and ate them on the short walk back to Dom's place.

There was indeed a Peter Fielder listed at an Arundel address in the BT residential on-line directory. I also checked whether there was a train connection to the town.

The phone rang several times and I had almost given up when a gruff voice answered. "Yes?"

"Is that Peter Fielder?" I asked.

"Who wants to know?"

"My name is Ian Fielder. John Fielder was my father."

"Never heard of you," he snapped.

I feared he might put the phone down before I got any

further. "Did you know he was killed earlier this year in a hit and run?"

A pause, "Yes, that's right," he said guardedly. "But I'm damn sure you weren't at the funeral."

"No I wasn't. I have only just found out that he had died."

"So?" He conveyed a lot of suspicion in that single word.

"My father left home when I was four. I never really knew him. I didn't even know I had an Uncle Peter. I have been working in Australia for four years. About six weeks ago he contacted me by email."

"That's impossible!"

"I know that now." I gave Uncle Peter a brief resume of the events that had let up to my phone call to him. "I really would like to meet you and try to find out more about my father."

Again he paused before replying. "When had you got in mind?"

"Today, if possible. I've only got a few more days in the UK. I can be with you by five o'clock this afternoon."

"Very well." Grudging acceptance but he gave me directions from the station to his cottage. Fortunately it sounded pretty close.

I told Dom that I was even more unsure whether I would be back later in the evening. I put a few things in my rucksack in case I needed to stay overnight and headed back to the station. I could pick up the Arundel train at Clapham Junction.

I was still hesitant about using my smart phone but there were things I needed to do that the cheap pay-as-you-go couldn't. Like surfing websites where I might discover more family history – or rather that of my father's side of the family.

A few minutes after the train had pulled out of Dorking my phone rang. Amy's mobile. I called her back on the burner phone.

"Ian, just to let you know I've taken your advice and I'm going away from Cassie's for the weekend. I'm on the way to the station now." Her voice didn't convey a great deal of enthusiasm. "Wish I wasn't on my own."

"It's probably for the best, Amy. Where are you going?"

"Cassie's booked me into a hotel in Brighton. It's not too far away from London, on the Sussex coast. She says it's quite historical. Georgian, whatever that means."

Without really thinking of the implications I replied, "I'm on my way to Sussex too."

"What!"

"Sorry, I shouldn't have said that."

"No, no, but I thought you were staying in London."

"I'm following up a lead."

"In Brighton?" she said, definitely with interest. "I'd be very happy for you to join me, Ian."

"Not Brighton," I said, then added "Even so, I'm not sure that would be a good idea."

"So where are you heading?"

I thought carefully for a moment before replying. I couldn't see that it would do any harm to mention my destination, though I held back from telling her the reason for my visit. Arundel was a fair distance from Brighton and it was quite possible I'd be back in London later that same evening. In any case, I'd more or less convinced myself that Amy had not been involved in any attempts to thwart my investigations. Or perhaps that's what I wanted to believe.

Chapter 8

Friday 2nd December : into the evening

My uncle lived just off the main street in a small terraced cottage faced with flintstone. Very attractive in a quaint sort of way. The man who came to the door was lean and tall. He'd probably been over six foot in his prime but now walked with a stoop. He had a couple of days' stubble and still had a thin covering of silvery hair above his large dark-rimmed spectacles. He was casually dressed in brown corduroys and a Fair Isle pattern pullover. I couldn't see any facial resemblance to my father as I had seen him on my laptop.

"Ian, is it?" he said.

I nodded.

"Before I ask you to come in would you mind showing me some confirmation of your identity – a passport or driving license? I'm sorry to be suspicious but I really don't know you from Adam. You can't be too careful these days."

Fortunately I had both documents with me.

"Thank you," he said. "I suppose I was aware that John had a son but I'm sure that we never met, even when you were a baby."

"And I wasn't aware until this morning that I had an uncle."

He led me into a cosy sitting room. A well-proportioned old lady sat propped up in an armchair, a scarf wrapped around her head and a zimmer frame parked by the chair. She was staring at a large television screen which showed Jeremiah Peel-Jackson, the new British Prime Minister arriving in Ottawa, the first stage of his grand tour of the Commonwealth countries. If he were visiting them all he could be away for the best part of a year.

"Elsie, can you please turn that off?" said Peter.

The screen died, and Elsie turned to look at me then enquiringly at Peter.

"Elsie, this is our long lost nephew, Ian, John's son."

A flash of recognition – or something – in her eyes and she held out her hand to me.

"Elsie can hear and understand everything we say but she's virtually lost the ability to speak. Cancer, I'm afraid. That's why she wears the scarf. The chemo has left her bald as a coot. And I always thought it would be me who lost my hair, like my father." Peter was much more relaxed and chatty now he was satisfied with my credentials.

"I'm sorry to hear that," I said, respectfully, taking her hand gently.

"Can't really complain, I suppose. We've had a good life." He directed me to another armchair the other side of the fireplace, in which an electric imitation log fire heater glowed warmly. "Now let's get you a cup of tea and you can tell me what you want to know."

Peter disappeared into the kitchen. I looked at the small framed photographs on the mantelpiece and a larger one on the desk in the alcove of two middle-aged couples.

"Is this you and Peter and my father?" I asked Elsie.

Her eyes lit up and she nodded vigorously.

I could recognise a younger Elsie and Peter and a family likeness between Peter and the other man, who looked nothing like the person with whom I'd been Skyping. He didn't have a beard though.

"Ah, right," said Peter, returning with teas and a plate of biscuits, "I see you've found your dad. That's his second wife, not your mother. She died a few years ago."

"Really?" I'd been under the impressions that it was more recent.

"Septicaemia sadly. John was devastated but he

seemed to spend even more time working after her death. We rarely saw him in recent years. Not that we were that close even before."

My fake father on Skype had told me that he had not had any children in his second marriage but I wondered whether that was true. I might have some cousins. There were none on my mother's side. "Did they have any children?"

"No. And neither have we. You're the only one left to carry on the Fielder name," he said with a twinkle in his eye.

"You mentioned that my father devoted even more time to his work after his wife died. So what exactly did he do?" A key question!

"Exactly? I'm not sure. He worked for some government department, I think. Quite high powered, I think. Often seemed to be spending a lot of time away. He never really talked much about his job."

"But was he still working up until his accident?"

"I presume so. He'd never talked about retirement, and he was of course quite a bit younger than me. Still in his fifties."

"And you are?

"My big seven-O next year. I took early retirement from teaching at sixty. To keep my sanity."

"Here in Arundel?"

"No, Chichester. An easy drive."

"Tell me, do you have any details about the accident that killed him?"

"Not really. He was walking back late one evening to wherever he was staying at the time, and a car knocked him down as he crossed the road. Sped away without stopping, and the couple of witnesses couldn't really give any description of the car or driver. Probably some yobbos high on booze and drugs."

"And the police never found the person responsible?"

"No, absolutely nothing to go on."

"Do you know where this happened?"

"Oh, somewhere in London."

"Lewisham?"

Peter shrugged, "Possibly. I don't know."

"But that wasn't where the funeral was held?"

"Oh no, that was at Lambeth Crematorium. Same as his second wife. Very low key."

I tried a long shot. "Going back to his work, I don't suppose you ever met any of his colleagues or friends?"

"They weren't in my circle of acquaintances." He thought for a moment. "There was this chap at the funeral. About the same age as John."

"You didn't get his name by any chance?"

"No, although he did speak to me briefly after the service. He probably realised I was family."

"Can you remember what he said?"

"Yes, strange really. He said he was so sorry to hear about old Bowler."

"Bowler? You're sure?"

"Yes, when I asked him, he said they'd been at school together, where, because of their surnames they'd been given cricketing nicknames by their classmates."

"What was this chap's nickname?"

"He didn't say. Didn't introduce himself at all, as far as I recall."

"Did you all go to the same school?"

"Yes, we both went to Lancing College."

My mind was racing with new speculations. And more questions that needed answering. There was only one, however, that Peter would almost certainly be able to answer.

"May I ask about the beneficiaries in his will?" I saw a frown pass over Peter's face. "Don't worry, I'm not intending to challenge it. I wondered whether there was anyone named that might be able to shed some light on what really happened."

"Sorry, Ian, I got the lot – not that it was very much at all really, since he didn't own a house."

We chatted for another half hour or so, mostly myself answering his questions about what I'd been doing with my life. He promised to keep in touch, and I in return promised to keep him updated on any further discoveries I made about John Fielder.

As I prepared to say farewell one more thought came to my mind. "Have you got a relatively recent photograph of my father? I really don't know what he looked like."

"Yes, I'm sure I can find one. Could you call by tomorrow morning for it? "

"Sure." That made the decision as to whether I was going to return to London straight away or stay overnight.

"You've got quite a lot of your father's features," Peter said as we shook hands.

Outside the air temperature in the chilly north wind was struggling to stay above zero. I needed to sort out somewhere to stay. Peter hadn't offered and I hadn't felt it appropriate to ask if they could put me up. First priority, however, was to get a good meal inside me. The Red Lion looked a good bet, with a sensibly priced menu. I'd barely sat down with a pint to make my choice when my phone rang.

"Hi, Amy." I'd recognised the number. "Safely arrived in Brighton?"

"No, I'm at Arundel Station."

"What?"

"I changed my mind. I really didn't want to be on my own in a strange town."

Christ!

"I hope you don't mind," she added apologetically when I didn't reply instantly."

"You are very fortunate that I'm not already on my way back to London," I said. It didn't come over particularly sympathetically.

"Oh … oh dear, I thought you would be staying over." She sounded close to tears. "I'm so sorry …"

"I hadn't actually decided." At that point. "Look, never mind. You're here now. I'm in the Red Lion, just about to order some food but I'll hang on until you join me." I hoped my voice had softened.

"Where is the pub?"

"In the town centre. You can't miss it. Just walk down over the bridge. It's up the High Street."

No sooner had I hung up than the phone trilled again.

"Ian, it's Dom. Are you coming back this evening?"

"No, there's a couple of things I need to do down here tomorrow. Why?"

"Oh, no problem. But I've found out some details of the hit and run."

"Go on!"

"Very late one evening in Ladywell Road – that's off Lewisham High Street. It was almost deserted. Two people saw what happened but they weren't very close. They heard a car rev up and it shot straight into him as he was crossing the road. No consistent description of the car, or numberplate. One witness thought there were two people in the car but couldn't be sure. Don't know how helpful that's going to be to you."

"Hmm." It appeared to back up what Peter told me. "Anyway, thanks, Dom, Probably see you tomorrow."

Dom's report made me even more certain that my father's death hadn't been an accident. Strange though that Lewisham Police hadn't made any connection between the hit and run and my enquiry about John Fielder.

A few minutes later Amy appeared at the door with a small valise, and looked nervously around the pub. Immediately she saw me she hurried over and flung her arms around me as I rose to greet her.

41

"Oh Ian, thank God! After I phoned you I realised how stupid I'd been." She sighed with relief. "I did it on an impulse. I felt as if I had been banished by you and Cassie. I haven't told her yet. I expect she'll be annoyed."

"Probably," I said, "but I'd leave off ringing her until the morning when we've got a better idea of what we're going to do next?"

"We?" she said. I detected some degree of optimism in her voice.

"Well, we're both here. We'll both be staying overnight now, I think. No way am I going to insist you go back to London or Brighton or wherever this evening."

"I'm sorry," she said again.

"I'm pleased you are here." Now I'd got over the initial shock, I was actually pleased to have her company.

"Really? You're not just saying that?"

"No, I do mean it. You really are a surprising person."

By the time we'd finished our meal, which was much more leisurely than I had originally intended, a band was setting up ready for a gig. While I would normally have been happy to stay and listen to live music all evening there was something more urgent to attend to. I did a search on my phone to see what accommodation might be available. Of the budget chains both a Comfort Inn and a Premier Inn were listed but on the outskirts of town.

When I returned from making my phone calls in a quieter part of the pub, I presented Amy with the options. I wasn't sure how she'd react to sharing a twin – the only room available at the centrally placed Norfolk Hotel – or taking the alternative of a long walk up hill past the station. Closeness of location obviously appealed to her and closeness to me a possible bonus.

The featured group were an Abba Tribute Band, which Amy suggested we listen to for a while since it would be only a short distance to our accommodation. Whether or not it was approved or intended by the management, two other couples took to the limited floor space and began to smooch around to a slower number.

"Shall we dance?" Amy took my hand before I could reply.

"I wouldn't have been doing this in Brighton," she whispered in my ear as we swayed closely together.

Chapter 9

Saturday 3rd December

For the second time in a week I woke up with the same attractive young woman beside me. On this occasion, however, we didn't have a cabin full of fellow travellers around us, nor were we restrained by seat belts. No restraints whatever had inhibited us after we had pushed the two single beds together by unspoken mutual agreement.

I gently removed Amy's arm from my shoulder and placed it across her bare breasts, then headed for the shower.

Undoubtedly I would have risen earlier had I spent the night alone.

It hadn't seemed appropriate the previous evening to talk further with Amy about my investigations but over breakfast I needed to decide an action plan for at least the next twenty four hours. It was obviously going to include her. While my gut feeling was that she was only an innocent bystander to the situation with my missing father and his imposter I still couldn't be one hundred percent certain that I wasn't being played. But if so she was an incredibly good actress and there were definite benefits in being able to keep a close eye on her.

It was now nearly a week since the Skype incident that had brought me to the UK. Although I knew a little more about my father, frustratingly, I was not much further forward in my quest for an explanation – just accumulating more unresolved conundrums.

Amy tentatively took my arm as we descended to the dining room. "Ian, I'm ... I shouldn't have..."

"No regrets for last night on my part," I said. Truthfully.

"I ... I thought ..." She paused, her thoughts unspoken. "Thank you, Ian. I've no regrets either."

I had to ask the difficult question. "Have you thought about what you want to do now?"

"Now?" she said innocently.

"I mean, after breakfast. The rest of the day. The rest of your time in this country."

"I'd like to help you."

I'd more or less expected this response. "I'm not sure how."

"You need someone used to digging through old files and documents. I work as an archivist in the library service."

"I remember you said you worked in a library." I thought about her offer and could see that with both her and Dom on board I could concentrate on following up direct contacts. "What about the rest of your holiday?"

"I'll still have some time after you've gone back to Sydney. With Cassie working I haven't really done much this week, except get involved with you anyway."

"It does seem strange that she invited you to stay when she didn't have time off herself."

"As she said, they're quite short staffed at the hospital and she got called back in to cover. She'd suggested a visit a couple of months ago but it was actually quite sudden when she sent me a text with a definite date when she was free – or at least expected to be. I'm quite lucky to be able to get time off whenever. Old files aren't usually urgent!"

Her mobile which she'd placed on the breakfast table started vibrating. She pressed a button to cancel the call.

I raised my eyebrows in question.

"Two missed calls and two texts from Cassie. She can wait a little longer."

Almost immediately the phone shook again.

"Oh hell," she said, "I suppose I'd better take it,

otherwise she'll be pestering all the time."

I couldn't hear what was being said by the caller but Amy pursed her lips.

"I'm in Arundel," she said curtly, and then after a short pause, "I changed my mind."

A further comment obviously irritated Amy. "You're not my mother, Cassie, I didn't want to be on my own. I'm with Ian."

She gave me a fleeting smile, then responded once more, "I know that was the plan but he's going to stay a few more days and he's asked for my help."

My turn to frown and she waved a finger at me and put it to her lips as she thought I was going to interrupt.

"I don't know, Cassie. This weekend, while you're still working. I'll still have some more holiday left." She sounded more conciliatory. "Look, I do appreciate your concern but I'm okay. Don't worry. I'll be in touch."

She terminated the call. "God, I didn't realise she was such a control freak."

"Patched up your differences?"

"Sort of. I would like to spend some time with her when you've gone back." She smiled at me "So what are we going to do today?"

Good question. "I'll call on my uncle again. He'll have a photo of my father that I need to show to some people."

Firstly, however, make contact with Lancing College. As I had expected with a boarding school there was someone to answer the phone on a Saturday morning.

"Good morning," I began, "my name is Ian Fielder. My uncle and my late father were students at Lancing College."

"Yes?" Curiosity or wariness in that single word.

"I am trying to trace an old school friend of my father."

"I'm not sure we can give out personal details. You would need to ask the Bursar on Monday. He's not here at the weekends."

"It's rather urgent. I have to fly back to Sydney on Monday." That was my original plan. I explained that all I was looking for was a surname of a contemporary of my father whose surname suggested a cricketing connection similar to my father's. A current address would of course be a bonus.

"I see." A non-committal response from the woman I was talking to. After a few moments, however, she came back with an encouraging response. "Look, I'm here in the office until one o'clock, and if you give me the appropriate years of attendance I may be able to find a register of students." As an afterthought she added, "It would be better if you can call in person. I'd be happier with that than giving the information over the phone."

"I'm not too far away, in Arundel. I can be with you by midday."

"Success?" asked Amy, as I terminated the call.

"Hopefully," I said. "I need to hire a car but I doubt if I'll find anywhere in Arundel. We'll pop round to my uncle and then head for the station."

Uncle Peter was prompt in answering the doorbell. He was surprised to see that I had an attractive young woman with me.

"You didn't mention yesterday you had a girlfriend with you." he said, casting an approving eye over her.

Yesterday I didn't. But I couldn't think of a suitable reply that would not have required further explanation, so I just introduced her, "Peter, this is Amy. She's from Melbourne." And left him to draw his own conclusions.

"Pleased to meet you," he said, and then to me, "Right, now I've got a couple of photos of John you can have, not particularly recent, but I don't think he changed much." He handed me a brown envelope. "You can keep them, I don't need them back. There's also this sheet of notepaper. I found it in a pocket of one of his shirts I brought back from his digs. I keep meaning to take them

47

to a charity shop. I must have put the paper with his photo. Probably thought it important at the time."

"Thanks very much indeed." I resisted the urge to examine the paper there and then. "I'll keep in touch with you." I thought of another question. "By the way, where were his digs?"

"Oh, some boarding house up in North London."

*****

We just missed a train. However, I had a chance to check on car hire firms on my phone, which was fortunate since the Europ Hire depot was closer to Lancing station, the next main stop beyond Worthing. I wanted to be able to return the car to one of their other bases, depending on where and when my investigations led.

I had a look at the photos Peter had given me. One thing was sure; the person who had Skyped me was definitely not my father. He was clean-shaven in all of the pictures, but of course he may have grown a beard since they were taken. .

"May I have a look?" Amy asked.

I passed them over to her.

"I can certainly see the likeness," she said. "Same shape face, almost square-jawed, same delicate nose, even the same dimple in the chin. When you reach his age your brown hair will probably also be grey."

"Thanks very much!" I said.

I also quickly looked at the sheet of paper, obviously torn from a pocket notebook. It had just a few scribblings and some digits which could have been phone numbers. I would need to study it in detail.

It was close to midday when we arrived at Lancing College. Amy was suitably in awe of its large chapel perched on the hillside overlooking an airfield and river.

I introduced myself and Amy to the middle-aged

woman in the school office. Mrs Bailey-Johnson, according to the sign on the door. I presented my passport as an indication of good faith in confirming my identity.

"John Fielder, you said was your father?"

"That's correct. His nickname apparently was Bowler and his best friend's nickname was also linked to cricket."

She chuckled, "We certainly have a strong cricketing tradition here. So you are hoping to find who he was?"

I nodded.

"Well, when you father was here, in the same year group, there are two clear possibilities – a Robert Driver and a Christopher Bateman. That's near enough to Batsman. No other names rang any cricketing bells but I'll speak to the Bursar on Monday morning and let you know if he has any other information.

"That's a great help," I said. "I don't suppose you have any current addresses?"

"No, I'm sorry. And I don't think I'd be able to give them to you anyway."

I had another thought. "Date of birth perhaps?"

"That I can do."

She gave me the relevant information and I thanked her profusely. I felt pretty confident I could find Bateman and Driver

Even though we'd had quite a substantial breakfast nearly five hours previously I suggested to Amy that we first had something to eat and drink. In any case I wanted to send the data on my father's classmates to Dom to see what he could come up with. We came off the A27 just across the river from the college and passed a rickety old wooden bridge. Amazing, I thought, that this had at one time probably carried the bulk of the main road traffic. We found two pubs nearby, and settled on the Amsterdam, which had more of a restaurant feel to it. As I was standing at the bar, waiting to order food and drinks I glanced at a television screen. It seemed to be on the local news channel and a reporter was standing with his back to the scene of a house fire. The sound was turned down so I couldn't hear what he was saying but I recognised the location. I had been there only a few hours earlier. Worried, I phoned my uncle – and got no reply. No dialling tone, number unobtainable.

I quickly rejected the idea of calling 999. The emergency from their end had already been dealt with. I tried the non-urgent police line, and explained my concern about what I'd just seen on TV. When I gave my name, the operator asked me to hold the line for a moment. She then confirmed my worst fears.

"The emergency services are attending a fire at the home of a Mr Peter Fielding in Arundel."

"That's my uncle!" I exclaimed, "Is he okay?"

Many more seconds on hold. "He has been taken to Worthing Hospital with critical injuries. A woman's body was recovered from the premises. I can also confirm that the police are treating the incident as suspicious."

I took several deep breaths. I didn't like the implications of what I had heard.

"May I ask where you are at the moment, sir?"

I'd forgotten that I hadn't terminated the call. "I'm in Shoreham. But I will be going to the hospital."

"Have you seen your uncle recently?"

"Yesterday afternoon, and again, earlier this morning."

"Then it is very likely the police will want to speak with you, sir. Can you please give me a contact number and address?"

I gave her my mobile number and hung up. I wasn't sure that a current no fixed abode would be helpful.

Amy was looking towards me, no doubt concerned that I seemed to be taking a hell of a time with the drinks. I held up a finger. I needed to think. I couldn't believe that the fire at Uncle Peter's was pure bad luck and coincidence. Yet who knew about his connection with me? Dom? – No way! Amy knew the address – but she'd been with me ever since we'd left Arundel. Unless …

I returned to where she was sitting, trying to look more relaxed than I felt.

"Problem?" she said.

"Something's come up," I said. "Look, can I borrow your phone to make an urgent call? Mine is running low on battery."

Her brows knitted for a moment, then she handed it over to me. "Shall I order while you make the call?"

I wasn't feeling hungry any more but nodded, "Just soup."

I checked through her log of calls and emails. Nothing outgoing since her calls to me yesterday afternoon and evening. But there was the incoming call from Cassie at breakfast. And Amy had definitely mentioned she was with me in Arundel. But surely … how could she possibly be involved?

Amy was returning with glasses. I quickly dialled Dom and asked him if he'd spoken to anyone else about my uncle, and he confirmed what I had expected – he hadn't told anyone else. He was puzzled why I had asked and I just said. "Explain later. 'Bye."

"Brought you a pint of Landlord? Is that okay?"

"Yes thanks," I said perhaps more curtly than necessary.

"What's up, Ian?"

I looked at her intently. "I wish I knew. I'm convinced my father was mixed up in unpleasant business, and whatever it was, it's putting me at risk – and anyone else I'm in contact with."

"Something else has happened, yes?" Her voice was tinged with fear. "Cassie? Your friend you're staying with?" She saw me shake my head. "Not … not your uncle!"

"After we left, there was a fire at his house. He's critical, in hospital."

"But …" I'm sure the look of horror on her face couldn't have been faked but implications were beginning to dawn on her." "You .. you thought I had something to do with it? Is that why you asked for my phone?" Almost snarling, her face twisted with anger.

"I didn't believe that you were involved in any way," I said calmly, "but I had to check."

She looked at me sullenly.

"I'm sorry," I said. "It's possible I was followed, or my phone has been bugged." It didn't seem the appropriate time to raise suspicions about Cassie

She didn't say another word until we had consumed our soup and roll.

"I suppose you want me to leave," she said, without looking up, "if you don't trust me."

"I don't want you to leave, Amy." I chose my words carefully. "You have my trust. But I'm aware that if you stay with me you are probably going to put yourself in danger."

She raised her head. "If what has happened to your uncle is anything to go by I'm likely to be in danger anyway just because I've been with you."

"I wouldn't disagree with that."

"Then I'd rather be with you than on my own."

"Thank you. I appreciate your decision."

*****

Worthing Hospital informed me that Peter was out of immediate danger but still in intensive care. Furthermore he had regained consciousness. The hospital had evidently given the same information to the police who were already talking to him when I arrived. A uniformed constable stood outside the door to his room. He suggested that we have a coffee in the cafe and he'd inform his superiors of our presence.

Amy was keeping very much to herself, with no attempt to chatter and fairly minimal responses to my attempts at conversation. I guess she was still miffed by my suspicions that she might have been in some way responsible for Peter's hospitalisation.

I took the opportunity to look again at the page Peter had given me. It was a jumble and torn at the edges. A few figures and abbreviations in capital and lower case letters that made little sense.

CsB? CS
wc co? or (page torn)
(page torn) PJ
(page torn) 0 ? x
128Cb?
1210S/Pm?
125 x 1212Bb

"Amy, what's Cassie's surname?"

"Married or maiden?"

"I didn't realise she was married."

"She isn't any longer. It lasted all of eighteen months. Must be a year or more since she left him."

I waited for her to continue.

"I think she's gone back to her maiden name."

"Which is?"

"She was born Casseiopea Byrne."

CsB was a very flimsy connection. However Amy's answer rang a completely different bell.

"You were friends at school together in Melbourne, right?"

"Yes, until we went our separate ways at University."

"So would you have known her parents?"

"Yes, of course. Why are you asking?" she asked warily.

I tried to sound casual, "Oh, no great matter, probably just a coincidence. My editor in Sydney is also called

Byrne. You don't happen to know what Cassie's father did for a living?"

"Never really gave it much thought. They were fairly well off though. He was definitely the executive or professional type, certainly not one to get his hands dirty or work up a sweat."

"Sounds as though you weren't impressed by him."

"Oh he was okay. Never felt I wasn't welcome in his home, but he came over as rather aloof and self-important. He did arrange the trip over here for me though."

"Really? Why would he do that?"

"Cassie asked him, I suppose. Anyhow I insisted on paying him back."

"Do you know his Christian name?"

"I always knew him as Mr Byrne."

"Can you describe him?"

"Look what is this, Ian? How on earth is Cassie's dad anything to do with anything?"

"He isn't," I said quickly, if not in all honesty, "I just wondered whether he could be my boss. It's a small world, you know, things like this do happen."

She appeared satisfied with my explanation, but any further response was left unvoiced, as two men came over to our table in the cafe. I guessed they were police officers before they even made their formal introduction as DI Rogers and DS Hyde.

"Mr Fielder?"

I nodded, and indicated the spare seats at the table.

"And your partner?"

Amy shot me a quick glance before replying, "Amy Cadwallader." Then added in a half-hearted attempt to dispel the idea that we were an item, "We're both from Australia."

"So I understand," said DI Rogers. "And I understand that you were both at the house of Mr Peter Fielder earlier this morning. Can you give me an account of the reason for your visit?"

I gave him an abbreviated account of what had brought me to my uncle's place, and back to the UK in the first place. He seemed quite taken aback by what I had to say.

"You can check with DI Myers at Lewisham Police Station," I said.

He pondered for a moment. "Your story all seems to hinge on a Skype message. Can you provide any evidence that this Skype conversation ever took place? I don't want to appear to doubt your word."

Which is exactly what he was doing. "I have my laptop with me. It should have the record of time, date and length of conversations, though I'm pretty sure that audio or video records aren't kept." Thinking about it, I wondered whether that was actually the case.

The inspector gestured that he would like to see for himself on my laptop. I fired it up and duly obliged. The last Skype conversation showed it had been terminated after only 4 minutes on the previous Sunday morning, Sydney time.

"Thank you," he said. And again stroked his chin in thought before continuing. "Let me see, you are thinking that your late father may have been involved in some business that attracted the attention of some very unpleasant characters, who are for some reason also pursuing you and other family members."

I nodded.

He went on, "And you think that is because these characters believe he passed on to you some information harmful to them?"

"That sums it up."

"You've no idea who they are or the nature of their business?"

"No." I could have added 'not yet'.

"If the incident with your uncle is, as you suggest, connected to you, have you any idea how they managed to track your visit to Arundel?"

I wasn't prepared to share my suspicions at this stage. "Possible monitoring mobile phone, though I have used it as little as possible, or perhaps they have been following me."

"So do you think they are still following you?"

"I really don't know. Since I hired a car this morning it would not have been easy to keep track of me."

He changed tack. "Tell me, did your uncle give you anything of your father's to take away?"

I wasn't sure what information they had been able to get from Peter. "A couple of photographs of my father," I said. "In an envelope."

"Nothing else?"

"No."

"May I see them?"

"Sure."I'd put the sheet of paper into my jacket pocket while I had been talking to Amy prior to his appearance.

He looked at the photos and handed them back.

I had a couple of questions for him "How is my uncle? Do you think the fire was arson?"

"Your uncle is very lucky to have survived. There is evidence that he suffered physical assault. It looks as if he was coshed with a handgun before the fire was started but regained consciousness in time to crawl out through the back door. He has some minor burns, and bruises and suffered some smoke inhalation,"

"Did he give any indication of what he had told them?"

"Photos. Photos. He was most insistent that he had given you photos. Which you have confirmed."

So, hopefully, nothing about the notebook or the mysterious schoolfriend. "Was he able to give you a description of his attackers?"

"Not terribly helpful other than white male, and local,

according to their accents. They were wearing masks."

"And my aunt?"

"Not so fortunate. Badly burned and still in the armchair in the sitting room. We are awaiting a post mortem report. Looks as if they doused the living room and hallway before they dropped a match and fled."

"Didn't anybody see them?"

"A couple of vague reports of two blokes speeding away in a car. Good thing is that the fire was reported promptly."

I wondered how Peter would cope with the loss of Elsie.

"May I ask what your plans are now, Mr Fielder?"

Quite a few different ideas were racing around my brain but as far as DI Rogers was concerned, I replied, "I guess I'll be returning to Sydney." But not when.

In all this time the junior officer had taken notes but had said nothing. As they rose to leave, he handed me a card and invited me to get in touch if I had any other information. I also gave him my mobile number on request.

Amy took my hand as I sat at the table, basically staring at the wall. "I'm sorry," she said softly.

"Not your fault," I said.

"I mean, I'm sorry for what you are going through."

"Thank you." I pulled her close and kissed her gently on the cheek.

We made our way back to Peter's ward. I wanted to talk to him to find out what information he had actually given to his assailants. However, the staff nurse politely told me that he was under sedation, and was not to be disturbed. When she suggested I call again in the morning I agreed but added that we had to be back in London this evening so would not be able to visit him again yet."

As we made our way out of the hospital Amy said, "Are we really going back to London this evening?"

Earlier in the day that had been my intention. "No," I replied.

Amy was puzzled. "So why did you tell the nurse that we were?"

"Purely by chance I saw on local TV that Peter had survived the fire and we got to the hospital fairly quickly. His attackers must surely also be aware by now that he is still alive and they might expect me to visit him if I were still in the area."

"But we are still in the area."

"Yes, but if they make enquiries at the hospital about visiting relatives they will be told that I've returned to London."

Amy shrugged her shoulders. I don't think she quite got the gist of my argument.

I had to consider the possibility that the hospital was already under surveillance. I looked to see if anyone appeared to be taking a particular interest in our presence. Outside it had started to rain so I took good advantage of the folding umbrella I'd brought with me to hide our faces on the way to the car.

I sat in the car for a few moments deciding where to go, until Amy came up with the useful idea of spending the rest of the afternoon in Worthing's public library. It was relatively close to the hospital, although I felt it prudent to move the car to less expensive parking. It gave me the opportunity of checking out several things on-line and also looking at the notebook page again. Amy offered to search local records and on the internet for further background on both Peter and John Fielder, as well as hopefully identifying a Batsman or Driver.

Time well spent, as it happened. When we left the library just before it closed for the day, Amy could barely contain her excitement.

"I think I've found a Batsman," she declared. "Robert Driver died several years ago, but a Christopher Bateman with the correct birth date lives in Morden, in Surrey. I've got an address and a phone number."

"Well done," I said, honestly. However I didn't want to share my discoveries with her just yet. I needed to think through the implications, if any, of confirming that Cassie was indeed the daughter of my boss, Howard Byrne. The study of the notebook has also suggested some further lines of enquiry.

I could tell that Amy was debating with herself about raising some other issue. "Penny for your thoughts?" I said.

"Well ... er ... about tonight."

"Yes?"

"We are definitely not going back to London?"

"Not until tomorrow."

"So are we ... are we having another night in Arundel?"

"I thought we'd try to find something here in Worthing."

"Sharing a room?"

"If you're happy with that, so am I."

"You're not afraid that I might strangle you in the night?"

I wasn't sure whether she was just trying to make light of my earlier unfounded suspicions of her actions. "You could have done that yesterday," I said, and added, "but at least I'd die happy."

Her turn to consider whether I was being serious. Then she broke into a smile and gave me a hug.

There were no doubt plenty of accommodation options in Worthing itself but they would not have been cheap. I found a small guest house just north of Worthing in the village of Findon. I paid cash and signed in with a false name as a precaution against the small chance that the opposition would still check for anyone registering under the name of Fielding. I let Dom know that I wouldn't be returning that evening. He had no further news for me.

After a modest evening meal, Amy and I were in mutual agreement to avoid talking about the recent days' traumas for the rest of the evening, in order to get some respite from them.

But it was not to be.

Half-past-eight in the evening. We had barely settled into our room when Amy's phone rang. I could see from the look of consternation spreading over her face that something was amiss.

I got her attention, "Cassie?" I whispered.

She nodded and started to speak into the phone. "I'm in … er …"

She looked at me for confirmation of our location. Urgently, I put my finger to my lips to warn her not to reveal our location and then mouthed, "Ring back," while drawing my finger across my throat then pointing at her phone to terminate the call.

She frowned, then spoke to Cassie, "Sorry, very poor connection. I'll ring you back." She turned to me in obvious frustration. "What's that all about, Ian? Cassie's in trouble. She's got a couple of blokes who forced their way into her house and won't leave until she tells them where I am."

"I'll explain in a moment. After I've made a call myself."

She tossed her head, turned her back on me and folded her arms.

I checked my phone and dialled.

"Is it possible to speak with Cassie Byrne, please?" Hearing the reply I had hoped for, I said, "Thank you. Don't bother to disturb her, it's not urgent." I didn't give my name.

"What the hell's going on, Ian. Who did you ring?"

"Lewisham Hospital. Cassie implied she was working nights over the weekend. She's at work now."

"What! But she can't be! She's just told me …"

Realisation of the possibility that Cassie may not have been entirely honest began to dawn on Amy.

"Amy, I was going to hold off telling you of my suspicions about Cassie until I was sure. I think I've just had that confirmation."

I carefully explained what had led me to believe that Cassie knew what was going on with regard to myself and my father and may possibly have been even more proactive. Her father might well be my boss. It might be her initials in my father's notes, and no-one else knew that I was in Arundel. I was pretty sure I hadn't been followed, despite what I'd told the detective.

"That's incredible," said Amy. She was visibly shaken by my revelations. "I can't believe Cassie could be involved! How would she have known your uncle's address?"

"Not difficult to put two and two together if she knew I was in Arundel. See if there was a Fielder listed in the directory, same as I did. She would have had to pass the information on to others in the area to actually intervene."

"But why?"

"My feeling is still that these people suspect that my father passed on information about them to me and to Peter."

"But why the fire?"

"Perhaps to destroy any damaging evidence that Peter may have held, knowingly or otherwise. They would be very unhappy to know that I've got a page from my father's notebook."

"Why would Cassie involve me?"

"I suspect that she intended to use you to keep a track on me. You said her invitation was very recent."

"Y ..es, as I told you, not more than two weeks ago. And ... how could she be sure I'd be sitting next to you in the flight – or even on the same plane?"

"Difficult but quite possible for someone with the

booking information to amend the seating allocation."

"That implicates Cassie's father!"

I'd had the same thought unless it was just a lucky coincidence. It suggested some detailed advance planning and of course raised the question of the precise timing of the abduction of my father figure. Howard Byrne had to be involved somehow, even if unwittingly.

"It may be that Cassie had some plans to make sure you and I met up. She would have known that I would be visiting Lewisham. If I had been taken out of the equation permanently then the two of you could have had the normal holiday you were expecting." I suggested.

"But she supported the idea of you and I avoiding contact. That doesn't tie in with what you are saying."

"At the time she was expecting me to return to Sydney or had further plans to remove me from circulation when you were out of the way. She obviously didn't expect me to dash off to Arundel, or for you to follow me."

"What do want me to do?"

I thought carefully before replying.

"Nothing. Cassie is not in danger even if she's worried about losing track of both you and me."

Chapter 10

Sunday 4ᵗʰ December : morning

Sunday was not going to be a day of rest. However, an early phone call to Worthing Hospital relieved me of one commitment I was still considering, despite my concerns about being watched. Peter had taken a turn for the worse during the night and would not be able to receive visitors. I said a silent prayer for his recovery and hoped that I would at some point be able to meet him again, or at least talk.

As we didn't have to head back into central Worthing, I rang Christopher Bateman who, fortunately, was willing to bring forward the meeting he'd agreed to when I'd contacted him the previous evening. He had been surprised by my call. Although he knew that John Fielder had fathered a son in his first marriage he declared that he was unaware that they were in contact with each other. Actually we weren't – but I held back from explaining the circumstances until we met face to face.

Amy was still concerned about what to do about Cassie. Almost as a matter of habit she'd switched on her phone at breakfast and found missed calls and texts from her, all appearing desperate and urgent.

"Text her. Tell her you left me in Worthing and you've gone to Brighton after all. And then switch off the phone!"

"Should I really go back to her place again?"

"I don't know. Presumably you've got some of your stuff there?"

"Yes. But I don't think I want to stay there."

I had some ideas about that but I needed to think through the best way of implementing them.

"Can you describe Cassie's house? Is it terraced, a semi

or what?"

"It's in the middle of a short terrace."

"Rear garden?"

"Not a garden as such but a rear yard and a shed. I think there's also a gate into an alley"

"Is her road a cul-de-sac or one way?"

"Er, no."

"You don't seem too sure."

"Definitely not a cul-de-sac. I've only been there on foot so didn't notice whether traffic could go both ways."

Checking the road atlas which I guess some previous user rather than the car hire firm had left in the pocket behind the front seat, I found that the A24 actually led to Morden. As far as Dorking the road was pretty fast, and mostly dual carriageway. Beyond Leatherhead, however, the journey became slower as we entered the suburbia of greater London with traffic lights ever increasing in frequency and a need to keep a close eye on the signposts as the main road was inclined to make sudden changes of direction rather than just going straight on.

Amy wanted to accompany me when I met Christopher Bateman. I wasn't sure whether that was wise in the circumstances since I didn't know the nature of his connection to my father other than as classmates. I suggested that she had a look around the shops.

"I don't know the place at all," she said, "I don't want to get lost. Anyway the only places open on a Sunday will be places like Aldi, cafes and takeaways."

I caught a glimpse of a Lidl in my mirror – a chain which, unlike Aldi, hadn't yet made it to Australia.

I could see that Amy was also getting fidgety. "What's up?"

"I'm still worried about Cassie. What if she's just being forced to … to get involved?"

I thought for a moment. "Possible, I suppose. One way to find out."

"What do you mean?"

"I want to talk to her directly." I didn't explain my reasons.

Reluctantly Amy agreed to wait in a cafe while I conducted the interview. I told her I didn't expect to be more than about half an hour, and would ring her to let her know when I was finished.

Christopher had given me an address which I had discovered was a residential cul-de-sac close to the centre of Morden. On a Sunday morning cars were parked on both sides of the road leaving just a single vehicle width access to the turning circle at the end, where his house was situated. The houses all looked relatively modern and well-kept, in keeping with middle-class suburbia.

"Come on in," said the portly gent who opened the door. "You must be Ian."

For his age, Christopher Bateman held himself upright and straight-backed. He was just under six foot. His square face sported a well-trimmed light brown beard, matching the thinning hair. Both had flecks of grey. He was casually dressed in brown corduroys, pale green open necked shirt and a plain freckled grey pullover which looked as if it had been part of his wardrobe for many a year.

The living room into which he led us carried an aroma of tobacco, presumably from a recently extinguished briar resting on an ashtray.

"I trust you'll excuse the casual attire. Glad to get out of a suit by the end of the week, so you'll have to take me as you find me." He spoke without any noticeable accent – the Queen's English of a well-educated professional gentleman, but not snooty or condescending.

"No problem. I appreciate you giving up your time to see me," I said.

He invited us to sit down on the ample sofa. "Tea? Coffee? Or perhaps you'd like something stronger?"

"Coffee would be fine, thanks," I replied.

He bustled off to the kitchen. I took in the surroundings. The room was furnished for comfort and practicability rather than for display. There was little evidence to suggest the influence of a woman in his life, not even in any photographs. The only females on display were in a couple of mounted portraits of aristocratic ladies from an earlier era. Through the windows I could see a well tended lawn and vegetable garden.

"Now, young man," he said, placing a large cafetiere with cups and a plate of chocolate digestive biscuits on the table, "what can I do for you?" He looked at me closely, "You do certainly have John's features."

Though I was by now well-rehearsed in telling the ever-growing saga of my adventures in the UK. and the reason for coming in the first place, I kept my account brief and relevant only to my reason for making contact.

Even so when I had finished, Christopher, who had listened intently with an increasing look of concern on his face, commented, "That's quite a story. How specifically can I help you?"

"Were you in regular contact with my father?"

"Not in recent years. We used to meet up occasionally but it certainly wasn't regular. Once a year perhaps, when our paths crossed. We didn't go in for formally arranged meetings."

"Did he ever mention me? Did you know he had a son?"

"I was vaguely aware that he had a child by his first wife but he never talked about you."

"Do you remember the last time you saw him?"

"Let me see, it would have been about a year ago."

"And what was the occasion, if you don't mind me asking?"

"Strange, really. It was an election campaign meeting by our new Prime Minister – though he was leader of the opposition then. It's not really my scene but he's MP for the next constituency and I thought I'd go along to get an impression of him. You can't go by the newspapers these days. Anyway, John was also there. We only met briefly as we were both leaving. I invited him to join me for a drink but he said he'd got urgent business elsewhere."

This seemed a convenient point to ring up my main question. "Do you know anything about the nature of my father's employment?"

"You think this all has something to do with his job?"

"I can't think of any other explanation."

"Well, you may well be right," Christopher pondered for a moment. "He never really discussed his work with me, but from the odd comment I picked up over the years, it seemed like government business but all pretty hush-hush. Can't quite picture him as a James Bond though. Anyway, even when he was married, he rarely seemed to be at home, I believe."

I'm not sure whether I was relieved to find my father was unlikely to have been involved in criminal activities or worried that his work was still going to have an impact on my life.

"You've no idea of the nature of his work? It sounds as if he may have been working undercover."

"No idea, sorry."

"I suppose I shouldn't ask, but I presume you are not in the same line of business?"

"Well, if I was I wouldn't tell you, would I?" Christopher grinned at some private joke. "No, I'm just an ordinary Art Historian. I did lecture for several years but nowadays I spend much of my time at the National Portrait Gallery looking at ancient high quality mugshots."

Although our business was pretty much concluded, I had a couple more questions.

"Can you confirm that you were known at school by the nickname Batsman?"

"Now that's a name I haven't heard for a while."

"And John was Bowler?"

He nodded.

"Do you know whether anyone other than yourself ever referred to him by that name as an adult?"

"I always called him John whenever we met up over the years and he always called me Chris."

"I understand you attended his funeral?"

"No, I didn't."

That took me by surprise. I couldn't think a reason why he would lie. "You knew he was dead, though? "

He nodded.

"Did you know he'd been killed in an accident?"

Christopher thought for a moment, a frown on his face. "Must have read something in the paper, I suppose."

I thanked Christopher for his time and hospitality.

I called Amy. It was a good three-quarters of an hour since I'd left her. I apologised, and arranged to pick her up.

Morden to Lewisham is not that far as the crow flies, and I'm sure that bird would get there far quicker than a motorist obliged to take the tortuous route through suburbia and the South Circular. Even on a Sunday with less commercial traffic on the road, I reckoned forty five minutes would be a conservative estimate for the journey time. I did toy with the idea of visiting the crematorium at Lambeth since it was more or less on the way but I couldn't imagine that a memorial stone to my father and stepmother would yield any vital information. I might pay my respects another day.

Since it was getting near to lunchtime when we left Christopher's house I suggested grabbing a bite to eat first. We'd passed a Harvester pub as we'd come into Morden. I could also talk over with Amy what I had in mind.

"Firstly, I intend to call on that old woman in Railway Terrace."

"Why?" Amy asked, with a puzzled look on her face.

"She may be able to identify my father as the 'young' Mr Bowler who lived next door."

"Right," Amy said, and then added after a moment's thought, "but that won't answer the question of who was Skyping you."

"No, but at least I will have established a plausible connection with Lewisham."

"And then?"

"I want you to show me the way to Cassie's house."

"But she thinks I'm in Brighton!"

"I want her to continue to think that – although it wouldn't take her long to find out that you still haven't booked into the hotel she had arranged. I'll say that you were worried about her and asked me to call when I returned to London."

Amy thought for a moment before replying. "So what am I supposed to do?"

"Stay in the car." I caught a quick frown. "Don't worry. I'm going to park away from the house, and I don't intend to be there long." I realised it was the second time that day I'd sidelined Amy.

"I'm concerned about what I'm supposed to do tonight – and for the rest of my time in the UK "

I hadn't really thought that far ahead. "Well, if Cassie believes that you and I are no longer together, then you wouldn't be under any threat on my account by staying at her place. And enjoy the rest of your holiday."

"You don't want to see me again?" Amy said indignantly. Her voice was rising. "You just want to get shot of me?"

She stood up quickly.

"Sorry, Amy, that's not what I meant." I hoped I sounded as contrite and apologetic as I felt. "I do very much want to see you again."

About to walk away, she paused, her lips pursed.

"That was just one option. Look, Amy, please sit down,

and let's look at other possibilities."

She took a deep breath and took her seat again.

"Well?" she challenged.

"I'm sorry if it sounded that I was giving you the push. The idea of you returning to Cassie's was not that we shouldn't meet, but that Cassie should believe we weren't seeing each other. The tables would be turned so that you would be keeping a check on Cassie on my behalf rather than the other way round."

"Ok...ay," she conceded.

"If you don't stay with Cassie, then I assume you wouldn't be happy going off on your own ..."

"Too right I wouldn't!"

"And you would want to be with me? Despite the fact that I don't know how things are going to work out here, how long I'll need to stay and what further threats to my safety – and yours – might arise?"

"Yes. And I'm good with the uncertainty."

"Thank you. I really appreciate your support." I took her hand.

She didn't object. "Let's see how things pan out this afternoon and take it from there.

Chapter 11

Sunday 4th December : afternoon

As I turned into Railway Terrace, I looked to see if any of the yobs who had attacked me a week ago were hanging around, though I suspect they were still hiding from the police. No-one had been in touch with me to make any formal identification so I assumed they had not been arrested.

I thought perhaps the old lady wasn't home, but after leaning on the doorbell for a second time I heard someone shuffling and calling, "I'm coming, I'm coming."

She opened the door and peered at me, "I've seen you before," she declared before I had a chance to speak, "Weren't you here last week?"

"Yes, I was indeed, enquiring about my father. I wonder if you could have a look at this photograph and tell me whether you recognise him."

She took the photograph from me and fumbled to put on her glasses which dangled from a chain around her scrawny neck.

"Why yes, that's Mr Bowler. He lived next door." She looked up at me as she handed the photograph back. "But that's not the name you gave me, is it? Fielder, wasn't it?"

The lady certainly had all her brain cells working.

"Yes, I've discovered that he was probably living under an alias."

"Not in trouble with the police, I hope. He seemed such a nice young man."

To her he probably was young, even though he was in his fifties.

"No, I don't think so at all. Tell, me can you remember the last time you saw him?"

"Oh, now let me see... er ...it must have been August ... no, no, it was after that, probably end of September, or thereabouts."

That tied in with the date of the 'accident'.

"Has anyone else been in the house since? As far as you know, of course." I didn't want her to get the impression I thought she was a nosey parker.

"Oh, a couple of chaps were there not long after. Spent most of the day there. There was a young woman with them. Relatives I suppose – but you'd know about that."

I didn't but refrained from commenting. They could have been police or his attackers but I'd bet my last dollar they weren't relatives!

"And that's it? No other visitors?"

"No, young man, I'd have noticed." She scratched her head, "But there was a break in. At least someone tried, but I heard breaking glass – my bedroom is at the back, you know – and I called the police."

"When was this?"

"Oh about a week after his family came."

"Thank you very much for your time. You have been very helpful."

"Thank you, young man. Tell me, do you have any idea what has happened to your father?"

"I regret to say he was killed in a car accident."

"I am so sorry, my dear."

*****

Amy could tell that I'd made some progress, "Good news?"

"It's him. She identified him as Bowler. She also told me that some people – relatives, she assumed – had been over the house. I'll need to check whether Lewisham police know about it."

As we waited by a set of traffic lights, I noticed a

billboard outside a newsagents proclaiming, 'Body of missing teenager found.' I didn't think anything more of it at the time.

Amy directed me on the short drive to where Cassie lived. I drove round the block to look for possible rear access – or egress – then parked about a hundred yards along the road from her house. The front entrance could still be seen. Amy had agreed to stay in the car for the duration of my visit, which I was not expecting to take long. I pulled my coat tightly around me against the bitter wind and set off.

I rang her doorbell a couple of times before she answered. She looked as if she'd dressed hurriedly. I'd probably either woken her or caught her as she was just getting up in preparation for her next night shift. Her surprise was evident.

"Ian? What … what the hell are you doing here? Where's Amy?"

"She asked me to call. She was worried about you," I said politely.

"So where is she?"

"Didn't she send you a message?"

"I've been asleep for the past few hours, in case you hadn't realised!"

"I can explain..."

"Oh, you'd better come in then, I'm bloody well freezing standing here at the door."

Me too, I could have replied. "Thanks."

I followed her into the hallway. A table with a large vase of artificial flowers stood just inside, next to a hat and coat rack, and beyond, a staircase. Cassie led me through a door on the left into a lounge diner that stretched from front to back of the house. Through the partly drawn curtains I could see the rear yard with a shed and a patch of grass. No rear gate was evident.

"Well?" She perched herself on the arm of the sofa

which had definitely seen better days.

"Amy's gone to Brighton, as you originally suggested, I believe."

"So why did she tell me she was with you in Arundel?"

"She was. Spur of the moment, curiosity, I suppose. I was flabbergasted when she called and told me she was at Arundel station."

"And why were you in Arundel?"

As she almost certainly knew already, there was no point in being evasive. "I'd discovered my father's elder brother lived there."

"Was he able to tell you anything?" Cassie made it sound like a casual enquiry.

"Not a lot, they weren't all that close. Confirmed that he'd died in a car accident, and gave me an old photo. That's all really."

"Do you mind if I put the kettle on? You'd like a cup of tea?"

"Yes, thanks."

She disappeared into the kitchen. I took a look at the couple of family photos on the mantelpiece. She returned a couple of minutes later with two steaming mugs.

"Wasn't that Friday you were in Arundel?"

"Yes but I had to pick up the photo on Saturday morning. I was then going to drop Amy off in Brighton before returning to London. By chance, I found out that, shortly after we had left, my uncle was attacked and his house set on fire. But you probably know that already."

Her reaction was defensive rather than sympathetic towards my relatives. She frowned. "Why would I?"

"It was on the news. "

"Don't watch it," she said tersely.

"It also seems a strange coincidence that he was targeted just after my visit. His wife – my aunt – died in the fire, and my uncle is critically ill in hospital. I spent most of yesterday in the hospital and talking to the police.

They also think there is a connection between my enquiries about my father and the incident. Only one person other than Amy knew I was in Arundel."

Cassie picked up the inference very quickly. "You haven't suggested to them that I had anything to do with it, surely?"

"No, I haven't – yet. In my line of work I tend to be suspicious about strange coincidences and things that don't quite add up but I don't pass on unfounded allegations."

Cassie glanced at her watch.

"I'm puzzled, for instance, why you misled Amy into thinking you were being held hostage."

"I was!" she declared vehemently.

"You were actually at work at the time. I checked with the hospital."

She couldn't meet my eyes. "I wondered who'd been trying to get in touch," she murmured, pursing her lips.

I changed the subject. "Your family?" I asked, indicating the photographs.

"Yes, my parents and brother. Why?"

"Your father is Howard Byrne?"

She nodded.

"He's my boss, but then I expect you knew that too."

Another confirmatory nod.

"Is your brother here in the UK as well?"

"No, but he did spend a couple of years in London doing postgrad. He finished last summer."

She looked at her watch again.

"Have you got a pressing engagement?" I asked. She didn't reply. "Look, what's going on here, Cassie? Nothing seems to make sense, and I seem to have been targeted ever since I came to London to find out what happened to my father."

I followed her glance out of the front window just as my phone trilled. Two blokes looking much like the bogus detectives were opening the front gate.

"You called them from the kitchen!" I shouted at Cassie.

I heard the front door open. I didn't wait for them to introduce themselves. I barged past Cassie into the kitchen hoping to find the rear exit Amy told me about. I leapt down the couple of steps into the yard and raced towards the wooden gate I could now see at the far end. Bolted! The bolt slid easily but the delay was all that was necessary for my pursuers to catch up. As the gate flung open, the back of my head exploded in pain.

When I came to, I was strapped to a chair in Cassie's living room. No sign of her.

The older of the two men, the one with the broken nose, faced me, sitting astride a chair, arms crossed on its backrest. "Perhaps now, Mr Fielder, you will feel more inclined to answer our questions."

I had a good few points of my own I wanted to ask about, but they would have to wait. Their questions, however, might yield some indication of where to focus my attention, assuming of course that my investigations were not terminated this afternoon.

"We want to know what information your father passed on to you."

"Nothing. I have not seen or spoken to my father since I was a young boy. I didn't even know he was dead until a couple of days ago."

His fist connected with my nose. "You expect us to believe that? Come now, you'll have to do better."

"I can't tell you what I don't know!" I gurgled, blood streaming from my nose into my mouth.

The younger bloke pulled a pair of pliers from his pocket and handed them to my inquisitor. "Perhaps we need to be a bit more persuasive," he said.

"What kind of information is he supposed to have given me?"

No reply. "Did someone else contact you on your father's behalf?"

"No! The only contact I've had I was from someone I now know to have been posing as my father. He enquired about my work, sort of casually, but never said what he did. And the reason I came to England at all was to try to find out why my so-called father was abducted before my very eyes while we were Skyping." I took a deep breath, "Would you know anything about that?"

He shrugged dismissively.

"You're a journalist, right?"

I nodded.

"You specialise in poking your nose into sensitive issues and embarrassing people in high places?"

Derogatory but basically a true description of the role of an investigative journalist. "If such people are abusing their position, yes."

"When did you start your latest assignment?"

"Two or three months ago." I presume he knew what the nature of the investigation was since he didn't bother to ask.

"Do you believe in coincidences?"

"They happen, but I am inclined to be suspicious. That comes with the job."

"We take suspicions very seriously. We believe your father, or someone working on his behalf, suggested a ... ah... a new focus for your work. Now we want to know exactly what you were told."

They were totally wide of the mark with the reason why I had begun looking at racist organisation in Australia, but it gave me a clue about my father's work. Not helpful in the immediate situation though. I replied quickly, "I was not told anything by my father, or anyone else in this country."

I flinched as I thought I was about to receive another blow but the man standing bent down to whisper something in his elder colleague's ear.

"Did your father's brother give you anything?"

Confirmation as if I needed it that they were connected to the Arundel incident. "Only a photograph," I lied.

"Nothing else? Nothing about your father's job?"

"Nothing."

They weren't happy. They hadn't got any information that they didn't already know. I wasn't going to be any use to them. I could recognise them, and connect them to my aunt's death. I wondered how they would organise my demise – slug on the head and turn on the gas? Arson again – or more direct action? And where was Cassie?

My captors were both standing now by the kitchen door. I couldn't overhear the instructions the older man was giving to his colleague. A look of consternation appeared on their faces as they turned at the sound of a siren. A police car with flashing blue lights screeched to a halt in the road outside and two officers were immediately out of the vehicle and making for the front door.

I guess my assailants didn't want to be caught red-handed for my murder. They bundled out of the back door. They pushed aside a plain-clothed officer who had come through the rear gate but their exit was blocked by two more policemen in uniform.

As an officer untied the ropes which bound me, DI Myers entered the room.

"Well, Mr Fielder, you do seem to be attracting a lot of attention from the wrong sort of people here in Lewisham."

I nodded.

"We'll need you to come down to the station and make a full statement about what happened here."

"There are some other matters I'd like to bring to your attention," I replied. "I'd prefer, if I may, to come down tomorrow morning. And I need to get cleaned up. My nose was still trickling blood."

She thought for a moment. "Ok, that works for me. Shall we say 9 o'clock? But please leave me your contact address and phone number."

Where I was going to stay tonight hadn't been in the forefront of my mind, and it of course might also depend upon Amy. Anyhow, I gave her Dom's address and phone. "He'll know where I am if I'm not there."

I was free to go. I splashed some water over my face and headed outside.

There was no sign of Amy or the car.

Chapter 12

Sunday 4th December : into the evening

Several possible scenarios went through my mind, most of which were not pleasant.

I fumbled in my pocket for my phone. Fortunately it hadn't been taken from me. No reply from Amy's mobile but I noticed a new text message and remembered my phone ringing just before I tried to escape. '2 men at Cs gate, x A.'

I left a message on her phone to ring me, soonest. I went back into Cassie's house and found DI Myers preparing to leave. She looked surprised to see me again.

"I left my friend in the car along the street. They're both gone."

"Have you tried ringing?"

"Yes. No joy. She's not answering. Tell me, how were you alerted to the incident here?

"One moment." She turned to a uniformed sergeant. "Bob, how did this call come in?"

"It was a 999 emergency call, ma'am. Apparently the caller was quite worked up."

"Male or female," I asked.

"Er, not sure, but I got the impression it was a woman."

Amy then, almost certainly. But where was she now? And, for that matter, where was Cassie? The thought struck me that Cassie could have looked at my phone while I was unconscious, as she would have heard the call too. It would have been easy to deduce that Amy was nearby, keeping watch — and Cassie had gone out to find her!

The inspector's voice broke into my speculations. "I think, Mr. Fielder, it might be better if you came back to the station with us now – particularly as you seem to be without transport."

"You're probably right. May I make a call to my friend first – the one whose address I gave you?"

"Okay, make it quick if you want a lift. We're almost done here."

I noticed that my two assailants had already been removed. I dialled Dom's number. No answer which was quite unusual for him. I left a message saying I hoped to be back at his flat tonight later in the evening.

Lewisham Police Station was only a few streets away. Although I had been there before I didn't remember passing it on the way to Cassie's. But one thing I immediately recognised. "That's my car!" I yelled. Parked between a police car and an unmarked saloon.

I was out of the car the moment it came to a halt and hurried to the entrance to the building, ignoring the calls of the driver to wait.

At the front desk, the walrus-moustached officer I'd met before was taking details from Amy, while another officer, probably from a patrol car, stood by her side. She glanced up, saw me and rushed into my arms.

"Ian, oh thank God you're here!"

I held her tight. "Glad to see you too." I turned to the traffic cop. "What happened?"

"Dangerous driving, no driving license, no insurance, no proof of ownership. Is it your car?"

"It's hired in my name."

"Then you shouldn't be letting your girlfriend drive it."

Detective Inspector Myers had followed me into the station and overheard the last exchange. "Leave it there for the moment," she said to the patrolman, and then to the desk sergeant, "Take a full statement but don't charge her. And bring her to my office when you're done." She indicated that I should follow her.

"See you later," I whispered to Amy as I passed.

We entered a small office, furnished with the basics but comfortably warm, and away from the traffic hubbub of Lewisham High Street.

"Well, Mr Fielder, perhaps you'd like to tell me how you came to be trussed up in that house," she began.

"Can I ask you a question first?"

"Go ahead."

"Was it Amy – the girl downstairs -who raised the alarm?"

"Probably, but we'll know for certain when we see what she has to say."

"Where would you like me to start?"

"The beginning would be a good idea."

"You are already aware of the reason why I came to London, from our earlier conversations," I said. "Since then there have been several developments. I've found my father was killed several weeks ago. I traced his brother and spoke to him just before he was attacked and his house set on fire. I've some idea about my father's line of business." I recounted in detail all the events that had happened in the past few days, including the names of the police officers who had spoken to me in Worthing, and my suspicions about Amy's friend." Which is why I went to see her," I concluded, "to find out just how she was involved."

"And did you find out?"

"Not entirely. I'm convinced there is a link. Its nature and reason I'm not really sure about though I have some ideas. Our chat was interrupted by the arrival of the two blokes you arrested. I'm pretty certain Cassie called them when she was in the kitchen. She'd disappeared by the time I'd recovered from being knocked out."

"Hmm, there's a bigger picture here that I'm not seeing." DI Myers rested her chin on her hands, in deep thought. "And where does Amy fit into all of this?"

I described our apparent chance meeting on the plane and her connection with Cassie from her schooldays.

"Do you suspect that she is actively involved in this … er … web of deception?"

"I did at one point, but I'm quite sure now that she's an innocent third party being conveniently used to keep track of me on behalf of her friend. It seems to have rather backfired on Cassie."

"Right, now I'm going to have to liaise with West Sussex Police over the events in Arundel since it seems that the men we have in custody – and Cassie, when we find her – may well be able to help with their enquiries."

"Have you by any chance found the youths who attacked me the other day?

She pursed her lips. "We've found a body which fits the description of one of your attackers."

That didn't make me feel any more secure. It reminded me of another question.

"I'd like you to look into another matter as well," I said. "You know I was looking for my father and you enquired about him in Railway Terrace?"

"Go on."

"I found he was living there under the assumed name of Robert Bowler. It seems he was the victim of a hit and run incident in Ladywell Road a few weeks ago. The driver responsible was apparently never found. Can you give me any more information?"

The inspector frowned. "Yes, I remember. Let me just check something." She picked up the phone and requested some details. After a couple of minutes she nodded, and said, "I thought so." And hung up.

"The whole case, including the handling of the corpse, was taken out of our hands by Special Branch. The demise of Mr Robert Bowler was not reported in the local paper."

"I see. That would in fact tie in with what I now suspect to be my father's employment based on what an old school friend of my father intimated earlier today."

"And who would that be?

"His name is Christopher Bateman. He lives in Morden."

"This seems to be something I'm going to have to pass up the chain," she mused.

Her comment triggered another thought. "Would it be possible for you to arrange someone from Special Branch to meet me? I've got some questions I'd like to ask."

"Mr Fielder, I think they will definitely have some questions to ask you!"

There was a knock on the door and on being invited to come in the desk sergeant entered. "Miss Cadwallader to see you, ma'am," he said, placing a document on her desk.

"Please show her in," said the inspector.

Amy still looked rather distraught, but she perked up on seeing me, and gave me a brief smile.

"Would you mind waiting downstairs, Mr Fielder? I won't keep Miss Cadwallader long but there are one or two things about your account that I need to confirm with her. I will arrange for someone to get in touch with you as you requested."

"Thank you."

I twiddled my thumbs as I sat in the reception area waiting for Amy and turning over the sequence of events in my mind. I realised I was still no further forward in discovering who had impersonated my father or why.

Some twenty minutes or so later Amy appeared. I stood up to give her a hug. She embraced me, trembling, and gripped me even tighter. "Oh God," she whispered.

"It's okay," I said gently.

"But what am I going to do tonight, Ian? I can't go back to Cassie's after what's happened ... and she's probably not even there!"

"Don't worry. Come back with me to my friend's house."

"Won't he mind?"

"Dom takes things as they come, but I'll give him a ring to let him know to expect company.

At that point it occurred to me that I needed to check the situation with my hire car. I hoped the police were not going to impound it.

The desk sergeant confirmed that I was okay to go. "The young lady won't be charged, in the circumstances," he said, as he handed over the keys, "just a caution."

Amy gave a huge sigh of relief.

"You can tell me about the circumstances on the journey," I said, "and I'll be doing the driving."

It was now early evening. We debated whether to stop for food before heading off or wait until we got to Barnes. We decided we didn't really want to hang around Lewisham any longer.

Whichever route I took it was going to be pretty slow and tortuous. As we'd already done a good chunk of the South Circular I headed towards the city and along the river via Chelsea and Fulham.

"I recognised the two men heading for Cassie's house," Amy began her tale. "I rang to warn you. I wasn't sure whether I should phone the police then and was still thinking about it when I saw Cassie hurrying out of the house and coming towards the car. She was looking at her phone but I didn't want to risk her seeing me, so I slid into the driver's seat, kept my head down and drove off. You'd left the keys in the car, fortunately. I didn't have a clue where I was going. I was trying to, kind of, go round the block but I got completely disorientated. I pulled over to look at the map but it wasn't much help. I saw a sign for Lewisham – God knows where I was at that point – and pulled across a lane to make the turn. Almost got rammed by a taxi which hooted like hell. It was then I realised I had the police on my tail. They pulled me over – and you know the rest!"

"So it was you that told the police about the danger to

me?"

"No , or rather, not until I got to the station. I didn't ring them."

I was gobsmacked. If not Amy then who? And why?

We drove in silence for a while. Until interrupted by Amy's mobile ringing.

"It's Cassie!" Amy exclaimed, looking at the number displayed. "Should I answer?"

I shrugged, "Up to you. But you might find out what she's playing at."

She paused for a moment then pressed the connect key and held the phone to her ear. "Hello, Amy here."

I could just about hear a voice on the other end but with the car engine and traffic noise I couldn't make out what Cassie was saying. She spoke for nearly a minute before Amy posed the question, "Why?"

"But Ian said you phoned them!" Amy insisted hotly after more lengthy chatter.

Amy listened again. "I'm really not sure whether I can trust you or not," she said eventually, and then almost immediately, "Why would I want to do that?"

Amy put her hand over the phone. "She wants to meet me to explain everything. She says she's been under pressure to follow instructions."

"From whom?"

"She won't say over the phone." She spoke into the phone again, looking at me for guidance. "Yes, I'm still here."

A short pause while Cassie spoke again. "Okay, but let me ring you back. Yes, yes, soon. Yes, this evening. Look, Cassie, I really need to get my head around what you are saying. Yes, I promise!"

Amy took a deep breath, and expelled slowly. "'Strewth!"

"Well?"

"Cassie claims she's been an unwitting – and unwilling

– accessory to whatever's happened to you and your father. She was horrified to hear about your aunt and uncle and blames herself. She says she didn't phone those men. She was expecting them to turn up again that afternoon. When they caught and tied you up she was afraid they were going to kill or seriously injure you. She got out of the house and phoned the police."

"What!"

"She sounds frightened. She wants to meet – both of us if possible, and tell us what she knows."

I was still suspicious. It could be another trap. Yet – if it shed more light on the situation …

"Ring her back. Suggest she goes to the police."

Amy dialled and conveyed my suggestion.

"She's scared to do that." Amy whispered to me.

"Just hold on a moment and let me talk to her."

I had just driven over Putney Bridge. I turned off the High Street and managed to find a vacant parking bay.

I switched off the engine and took the phone from Amy. "Hi Cassie. I think we do need to meet and talk. I think you would also be wise to tell the police what you know. But that can wait until tomorrow. For the moment, it would help me understand if you could tell me how you – and Amy – got drawn into my affairs. Was your father involved?"

I thought she wasn't going to answer. The phone seemed silent for a long time before she spoke. "I asked him if he could book a flight for Amy to visit. She's one of my oldest friends from school."

"When was this?"

"About two weeks ago. I'd arranged to have some time off. I thought with Amy here I could get away for a few days from all this... this business"

"Have you had any contact with your father more recently?"

"Yes, last Sunday. To tell me which flight Amy would be

on. He also mentioned that one of his journalists was travelling too on family business. That was you, I suppose."

"Yes." Another question occurred to me. "Tell me, what made you decide to come to London to work?"

"To get away from my ex-husband. But he's found out where I am."

I wanted to ask why – as well as a good many other things but that could all wait until tomorrow when I hoped she'd be able to explain her apparent involvement with subsequent incidents.

"I don't know quite what we've got mixed up in, Cassie, but perhaps you can tell me more of your side tomorrow."

Another pause, "We could Skype instead." She sounded hesitant.

After my previous experience with Skype that wasn't something I was keen to do. I'd rather see her face to face and be sure that she wasn't being directed by someone out of my view. I still wasn't entirely convinced that she was as innocent as she wanted me to believe. Even if she were telling the truth I didn't really want an obvious connection to me should anyone get access to her laptop.

"I''d prefer that we meet," I said. Then I took a chance. "I'll give you my email but please delete any messages after sending." I explained why. "May I suggest we meet again tomorrow at Horniman's, say, midday in the cafe? "

"I suppose so," she said reluctantly.

When she rang off, I wondered whether I'd actually blown my chance to find out what was going on.

I made one more call. Jayne Myers was no longer at the police station but I left a message to say I'd be meeting Cassie and thought that some covert police observation would be advisable.

I realised I was starving. We popped round the corner to a takeaway in the High Street. I also bought some bottles of beer. I knew Dom wouldn't turn his nose up at free food and booze.

I remembered something I had meant to ask Cassie.

"Amy, what was Cassie's married name?"

"Saunders. Charlie was a friend of her brother. Arrogant bastard thought he was God's gift to humanity. I didn't like him."

That name rang a bell. I had come across a reference to a Charlie in my investigations back home. I'd got the impression that it was a code name for one of the covert ultra-right cells I believed were operating – but it could have been a key person in that group. I guess, however, like any other English speaking country, Australia had its fair share of Charlies.

Chapter 13

Monday 5th December : morning

Dom, as I had expected, had taken the appearance of an extra guest without any undue concern or comment. He'd shown more interest in the beer and Chinese takeaway. Amy, however, had shown unexpected modesty in declining to share a room, let alone a bed, with the result that I'd spent a rather uncomfortable night on Dom's sofa.

She seemed quite cheerful at breakfast, and whispered to me, "Sorry about last night, Ian, it just didn't seem right to, well, take advantage of your friend's hospitality."

"No problem," I replied. I knew Dom wouldn't have been the slightest bit concerned what we got up to but I wasn't going to argue the point. Perhaps tonight, if we were both still here, we could come to a mutually acceptable arrangement.

"Hi, both. Sleep well?" said Dom, breezing in from the kitchen.

I was about to call on his goodwill again. "Dom, is it possible to retrieve any videos of Skype conversations?"

"I'm not sure. I know Zoom has a record facility which of course has to be switched on. I can check, if you leave your laptop with me, I'll see what I can find."

"Do you need the password?"

He grinned. "Not really, but it will save me a few minutes if I have it."

My phone rang. Still only 8.30 in the morning.

"Jayne Myers here. I've arranged for a Byron Masefield from Special Branch to meet you this morning. He'll be in touch."

"Okay. Did you get my message I left yesterday evening?"

She sounded surprised. "No, what was that about?"

I suppose she hadn't gone through all her messages yet. "I was contacted by Cassie – Amy's friend at the house where you found me. She wants to explain to both of us what happened. I was going to meet her and I'd asked if you could provide a discreet police presence as I'm suspicious of another trap."

"Where will you meet?"

"The cafe at Horniman's Museum. Midday."

"It might be best to make it a little later if possible. I don't know how long you'll need with Masefield."

"I'll try to reschedule for 2 pm and let you know if there's a problem."

"Okay. I'll have someone there." She rang off.

I tried ringing Cassie but got her messaging service. "Ian here. Sorry Cassie, another urgent meeting this morning. Can we make it 2 pm instead? Let me know."

My coffee was getting cold. I got one slurp in before my phone once more demanded my attention.

"Ian Fielder?" A female voice which sounded vaguely familiar.

"Yes, who's calling?"

"It's Fiona Bailey-Johnson, from Lancing College. There is another possible name. The boy joined the class part way through the year, so I didn't have his name on the list I looked at on Friday."

"What is his name?"

"It's Malcolm Wickens. Wickets, you see?" She gave me his date of birth.

"Yes, indeed. Thank you very much indeed for your trouble."

I rang off, then looked at my phone and noticed I had a missed call. I didn't recognise the number, but called anyway.

"Masefield."

"You rang me, Ian Fielder."

"Yes, thanks for calling back. I'm Detective Sergeant Byron Masefield. You have some information for me, I believe."

I hope the exchange of information would work both ways. "Yes, indeed."

"I can meet you at the address you provided at ten o'clock if that's convenient."

"Um." I didn't think Dom would be too happy to have a spook encroaching on his computing domain. "I don't really want to inconvenience the friend I'm staying with. Could we meet somewhere else?"

"Would you be prepared to come to the nearest police station? That would be Hammersmith."

"Yes, that's okay with me."

My phone now showed a message from Cassie. Brief. "OK."

I told Amy of the change of plans. "What do want me to do?" she said.

"Well, I've got another name for you to check, or you could come with me, but I doubt if you'll be able to sit in on the meeting. He might want to talk to you too, perhaps." I refrained from suggesting again that she could go shopping. She wasn't into retail therapy.

"She could have a look around the Wetland Centre just up the road," Dom chipped in.

It looked pretty cold and wet outside. Not tempting for an outdoor activity.

Amy decided to stay indoors. She said she would try to find out more about Wickens and Cassie's ex – with Dom's help, no doubt.

From his cultured voice on the phone I'd conjured up the mental image of Byron Masefield as a rather formal establishment upper class gentleman appropriate to his bardic names. I wasn't expecting the hirsute and casually dressed lanky fellow who greeted me at the police station, with a handshake and, "Hi, I'm Byron, and you are Ian?" I felt a bit silly asking to see his card just for confirmation.

He took me into a small interview room. "Sorry about this, it's all they could let me have. Coffee? I'll warn you it's from a machine."

"I'll pass, thanks."

"Right," he said, when we'd pulled up chairs to the bare table, "before we start, are you happy for this conversation to be recorded?"

"I've no objection."

"Just to confirm some details, then, you are Ian Fielder, an investigative journalist, working in Sydney, but originally from the UK?"

"That's correct."

"And your current area of investigation?"

"Far right groups in Australia."

"Was that your choice of topic?"

"Pretty much so." I told him about the assault on my coloured neighbours back in August.

"This was approved by your editor?"

"He gives me pretty much free reign, but, no, he didn't raise any objections."

"Now I've heard the basics of your story from Inspector Myers, but I'd like you to start at the beginning and bring me right up to date. Take your time."

Once again I went through the whole rigmarole from the initial contact supposedly from my father through to my conversation with Cassie the previous evening. Byron was very patient. He didn't interrupt once, though he made the occasional note on a pad. By the time I'd finished I was grateful for the water which he'd brought in, in lieu of coffee.

"Thank you. That was very thorough." He stroked his chin. "Now, you say the reason you came here was to investigate your father's apparent abduction."

I nodded.

"And you had no reason to believe it was connected in

any way with your own work?"

"Not then, no."

"So what particularly has let you to suspect otherwise?"

"Several things. Firstly I discovered my father had already died in suspicious circumstances before he made contact with me. I don't believe in ghosts."

Byron smiled.

"The attack on my uncle, hints that my father was involved in some kind of undercover work, and the thugs who held me obviously believed that my investigations in Australia may have started because of something my father passed on to me. And, retrospectively, the fact that my attackers on the first day were known to the local police as members of the English Defence League. You know, I suppose, that one of them is dead?"

"Yes, we know."

"Before we continue, can you confirm that my father was working for you?"

"That's not the kind of information we would normally make public, but in the circumstances ...yes, he was one of our top undercover agents."

"Was he also looking at the far right groups?"

"Initially, no. It was a more general threat against establishment figures – The government, politicians, the Royal Family – from some of the more way out and violent extremist groups, but with the change of government it became more focussed on a previously unknown organisation. Very low media profile, very well organised and very well financed. We believe they represent a real threat to our country."

I expressed my suspicion that there was a similar covert organisation in Australia. "Does this group have a name?"

"I'm not at liberty to divulge that information."

Pity, but not surprising. I remembered something

Christopher Bateman had said. "Was news of his death ever published in the newspaper?"

"No, not as Robert Bowler, nor as John Fielder."

"So how did his brother know?"

"John had left with us details of his brother and some other people to contact in the event of his death. He insisted his brother knew nothing at all about any of his work."

"He didn't leave details of his son – me?"

"No"

"As I have told you, my father never made contact with me, although his enemies, presumably this group you mentioned believed he had. But did any of his colleagues – your colleagues too, I suppose – try to contact me by email and Skype?"

"Categorically, no."

The most logical explanation for the Skype deception killed off.

"Can you confirm that my father was operating under the name of Robert Bowler?"

"That was one of his aliases."

"Do you believe that somehow his cover was blown and that he was killed as a result?"

"That seems very likely." He thought for a moment. "Have you any theories as to why Peter Fielder was attacked?"

"I presume they thought he might have passed on some information to me."

"But apparently he told them he'd only given you photos. He held something back, didn't he – perhaps to protect you ?"

"Yes. He gave me a sheet of paper which was among some of my father's clothes that Peter collected from a lodging he was using in North London." I handed it over. I had already made a copy of its contents.

Byron's faced creased in annoyance. "Bugger! We

searched the house in Railway Terrace top to bottom looking for something like this. He hadn't even told us about another dwelling." He looked up at me sharply, "Why didn't you hand this in before?"

"I've barely had the opportunity to do so, and I wanted to have a look through it myself first. Not that I found anything apart from a couple of initials that might or might not have referred to Cassie and her ex-husband."

"I'll keep this, if you don't mind."

"Okay." As if I had a choice.

"Did Peter give you anything else you haven't mentioned?"

"No."

"No names?"

"No, apart from the Bowler nickname."

"And you then traced the person who may have had the paired nickname of Batsman? This Christopher Bateman."

"Well, yes, or rather Amy did. But we did meet. He confirmed, or rather intimated, that my father was involved with the secret service or something similar."

"Do you think your father was beginning to have some suspicions about him but had no proof?"

"I don't know. Possibly. Do you think he could have had my uncle killed?"

"Perhaps. If he was involved, and the Bowler name your uncle mentioned enabled you to track him down, he may have thought that both Peter and Ian Fielder presented a very real risk to his position and took action accordingly."

"I hadn't thought of that," I said genuinely.

"Well, thank you very much, Ian, you have been most helpful," he said, offering his hand.

"Thank you for your time," I reciprocated. "Er, what now? Will you need to speak to me again? I am meeting with Cassie this afternoon and she told me she is prepared to share all she knows."

"Yes, I was aware of that meeting. Let Jayne Myers have a report." He paused. "Are you now intending to return to Sydney? You seem to have found out pretty much what you came for."

Except who made the Skype call. "I'll see. One or two loose ends, privately, to clear up then, yes, I suppose I'll head back home."

Cold and damp as it was, I was pleased to get outside in the fresh air. I was parched, and hungry. Altogether I'd been with Byron Masefield for nearly two hours.

I rang Dom "Would you and Amy care to join me at The Waterman's? I'll be there in about fifteen minutes.

On the bus journey I called Worthing Hospital. Something I had been meaning to do yesterday. The girl on reception put me on hold while she made enquiries about Peter Fielder. After a minute I was put through to the ward sister, and again introduced myself. She told me that my uncle was, thankfully, still in the land of the living, and was in a stable condition, though not yet out of intensive care. She also confirmed that there was still a police presence, which I was pleased to hear about.

"Is he awake?"

"Yes, he's just about to have his lunch."

"Is it possible to speak to him?"

"I'm sorry, that is not possible."

"Could you ask him a couple of questions for me, then? It's very important. And give him my best wishes."

"I'll see what I can do."

I described Christopher Bateman's appearance. "Ask him if this was the man he spoke to at the funeral, and if his attackers mentioned the name Bowler."

"Bowler? I'm not sure whether he will want to bring back such memories but I will speak to him."

A short wait, then the nurse answered, "Yes, they did, and he did not recognise the description of the man."

Chapter 14

Monday 5th December : afternoon

"I've found Malcolm Wickens!" Amy declared excitedly when I met her and Dom in the pub.

Given that Bateman appeared to be telling the truth about non-attendance at my father's funeral, Amy's news was welcome.

The downside was that his current address was in Bristol. It might as well have been Timbuktu for all the chance I had of arranging a face to face meeting with him in the short time I expected to remain in the UK. Fortunately, with Dom's assistance, she'd also obtained a telephone number.

A woman answered.

"Is it possible to speak to Malcom Wickens?" I introduced myself. "I believe he was at school with my father, John Fielder."

"Yes, that's right." She paused. "He died recently. My husband was determined to go to his funeral."

Bingo! "Can I have a word with your husband?"

"You can, but I must warn you he is in the early stages of Alzheimer's. He tends to get confused easily but he's still able to hold a conversation. Wait a moment."

I could hear her calling to her husband, and soon he took up the phone. "Malcolm Wickens here. You're Old Bowler's son?"

I could have terminated the call then as I'd got pretty much all the answers I required, even without asking the questions.

"Yes, but I never really knew him. He left my mother and me when I was still a toddler. I only found out last week that he had died."

No response, so I continued. "Did you know my father well?"

"Oh, yes, we've been friends ever since our schooldays. He was the first friend I had at my new school."

"If he was known as Bowler, was your nickname Wickets?"

"Why yes, how did you know that, young man?"

It would take too long to explain. "Was there anyone else with a cricketing nickname?"

"Mmm, let me think... Yes, there was a Batsman as well. Can't remember his real name."

"So you haven't kept in touch with this Batsman?"

"No, just the bowler," he chuckled.

"Do you know anything about my father's job? I'm really trying to get to know him, even though he's no longer with us."

"Same as me. Though not really. I was in the army – the military police, and he was up in London, in plain clothes. He didn't ever say much about what he did exactly."

"Thank you very much for your time."

"What did you say your name was?"

Over lunch Dom told me he hadn't had time to look at my Skype records. "Had some work to do – paying work," he'd added, pointedly. He'd rolled his eyes when I asked him, if he'd got the time, of course, to see what he could find out about Christopher Bateman, Cassie and her brother. I didn't bother asking him to do a further check on Malcolm Wickens. I couldn't really see a man with dementia problems being a mastermind of a conspiracy.

I debated whether to take the car with me to Lewisham but I didn't really see any point in running up hire costs unnecessarily. Although I'd found Europ Car had a depot in Putney near the tube station I thought we would be running too short of time to drop it off on the way to meet Cassie. I suppose, in retrospect, I could have dropped it off the previous evening and got the train back from Putney. Anyhow I rang them and paid a little extra for someone to collect it from where I had parked it. There had been no space at all in Dom's road and I had been lucky to find just one bay in the next street. I gave Dom the keys.

We arrived at the Horniman about ten minutes before our agreed meeting time. The cafe was almost empty – one family just finishing their meal, an old couple huddled in one corner and a young chap reading a newspaper, with a coffee and croissant on the table. No sign of Cassie.

I asked whether she had looked round the museum after I had left them on the previous occasion.

"Yes, some of it, but Cassie had to get back home and get ready for work, and I gathered up a few things and headed for the station."

While we waited we began chatting about our childhood and teenage memories.

"Why did you decide to move to Sydney?" Amy asked as our conversations got closer to the present.

"I had a couple of friends and a colleague who had moved there and really liked the lifestyle. Much more laid back than London. I didn't have any family back here, I was getting a bit fed up with my job as a junior crime reporter for the BBC, and I was looking for a change."

"But you didn't start working under Cassie's father, did you?"

"No, I was with the Herald for a while. Got a bit of a taste for probing into dodgy dealings. "

One cold coffee and half an hour later, Cassie still hadn't appeared. With the passing minutes we were both getting anxious.

"How long should we wait?" Amy said a few minutes later.

I shrugged. I was becoming resigned to a no-show.

"I'll give her a ring." Amy fished in her handbag. "She may have been held up," she added unconvincingly. She looked at the screen. "Oh! ... Ommigod!"

"What's up?"

"Cassie! She's sent a message! Oh God! My phone had got set to silent mode."

"What does she say?" Like Amy, I was worried.

"Here, you can see." Amy handed me the phone. She was close to tears.

'It's him. Police. Scared. Look me up."

"We must get to her house! She's in danger ... she's asking for my help!" Amy was beginning to panic.

The message seemed strangely worded. If it was bona fide then there was reason to act swiftly- but there was still an element of doubt in my mind. The message time was quite recent; it had been less than two hours earlier. Cassie would have been getting ready to leave the house to meet us.

"Just a moment, Amy. I'll be right back."

I walked quickly over to the table where the young fellow was still reading the newspaper. "Excuse me," I said, "May I ask if you are here at the request of Jayne Myers?"

He blinked in surprise, and then nodded. I beckoned Amy over

"I think we have a problem," I showed him the phone message. "This is from the person we were to meet. The message may or may not be genuine but either way, it's vital we check."

He pulled out his phone and made a call. "I've asked for someone to investigate immediately."

"If you are heading back to the Police Station can we come with you?" Amy pleaded. "We must see her!"

He looked undecided. Normally he would be the one inviting people to accompany him. "Okay," he said, "car's outside."

I was not looking forward to what we would find. Amy was trembling, and sat close to me on the back seat.

My phone rang. Dom. "Ian, something's happened!" I'd never known him sound even mildly agitated. "There's been an explosion. Just after I handed over the car keys. I'd only just turned the corner when I heard and felt the blast. Your hire car."

"What!" Unbelievable. "Are you okay?"

"Yes. Shaken though." As he sounded. "Driver not so lucky. Blown to kingdom come. Some pedestrians nearby injured and several cars and houses damaged. Shattered windows." I heard him take a deep breath. "Can you get back over here? The police will want to talk to you as you were the last person in the car."

"I'm with the police at the moment, on the way to Cassie's" I said, "She didn't show up and we think she may have come to harm."

"Oh yes, one other thing," said Dom. "There's a really weird email from her on your laptop, came early this morning. Doesn't make any sense."

"What does it say?"

"I'll copy it over to you. It's very short."

It was indeed short, and cryptic. *'Stick withall. Amy if SOS look me up C'*. Cassie obviously wouldn't have sent a trivial message but I couldn't fathom out what she was trying to say. It had that same odd way of asking Amy to call on her. I showed Amy the message and relayed what Dom had told me.

"Ian, I'm ... I'm scared. Someone tried to kill you! And it could have been both of us!"

Truth to tell, I was getting bloody scared too. Two attempted murders and a beating.

'Stick withall' Was she trying to tell me to stick with the investigation regardless? I tried to give some logical thought to Cassie's message. She apparently had information that I wanted. She had been prepared,

reluctantly, to meet. She'd felt under threat. I'd advised her to be cautious with email contact. '*Stick withall'* Could it be '*stick with all' information* ? A USB data stick perhaps? If anyone broke in looking for information she could not easily hide a laptop or even a mobile phone but it might be possible to conceal a small USB device. Where, though? On previous messages she had used A and C as abbreviations for both Amy and Cassie. '*Amy look me up C'* still didn't make much sense – we'd already looked her up, so to speak. Unless... I had a bizarre idea.

We arrived at Cassie's house just as an ambulance turned into the other end of the road. A squad car was already there.

Amy made to rush into the house but was held back by a policeman at the door, "Sorry, miss, you can't go in."

I caught up with her, and persuaded her to step aside with me for a moment. Quietly, to avoid being overheard, I shared my thought with Amy.

She was shocked "You can't be serious!"

From my expression she could see that I was deadly serious.

The paramedics, one male and one female, arrived and entered the house with a stretcher.

DI Myers came to the entrance, looking grim.

"What's happened?" I asked.

"She's taken an overdose. She's still alive ... just. It looks like suicide but we will be treating this as a crime scene. Someone's been in here and ransacked the place."

Amy collapsed in tears.

I told her about the message Amy had received. "Which is why we came straight here," I said.

"We found no mobile phone nor computer."

I chose my next words carefully. "Inspector, I believe Cassie has a USB stick with some information she wanted to share with me. I have a good idea where she has hidden it. It's very urgent, not least for my own safety, that I see that information as soon as possible. If I'm right the stick would be found but perhaps not for a couple of days. I will tell you now if you can guarantee that I have access to the information addressed to me."

She eyed me warily. "I'm not sure what you mean."

"Please, a delay might cause more deaths."

"Very well," she conceded. "Where do you think this USB stick is hidden?"

I told her. Her eyelids nearly flew off her forehead. "Wait here!" she commanded.

I put my arms round Amy while the inspector disappeared inside the house. A few minutes later she reappeared, and held out a small resealable plastic bag containing a USB data stick.

"You were right, Mr Fielder. I will need to keep this original but if you come to the station I will arrange for a copy of its contents to be made for you."

"Thank you. There is something else which I need to bring to your attention, if you have not already been informed."

"And what would that be?"

"The car that I hired – and was here yesterday – was blown up this afternoon, killing the driver who had come to collect the keys I'd left with my friend at lunchtime. That could have been me in the car."

"I hadn't heard. You believe you were the target?"

"Probably. I'd left the car in a neighbouring street to my friend's house last night."

"So someone knew where you were staying?"

"I don't think so."

"So how do you think the car was targeted?"

"Several people could have known that I had hired that car."

"But not where it was parked overnight?"

"That's true," I said, "Unless it had been fitted with a tracking device...." She wasn't going to like what I said next. "The only time it had been left unattended in the past twenty four hours was when it was sitting in the car park of your Police Station. And I left a message there for you about my intended meeting with Cassie today."

"Are you suggesting...." DI Myers began, and then realised that what I was implying could indeed be a logical explanation, even if unlikely. "Leave that with me!"

The paramedics brought Cassie out on a stretcher. She had an oxygen mask over her face. Amy turned away. If Cassie failed to recover, I realised I might have the difficult task of informing Howard Byrne of his daughter's death, and that it was very likely to have been linked in some way to my presence in London.

"Ian," Amy said quietly, "Do you think they'll let me collect my things from here? I can't face coming here again without ...without Cassie." She blew her nose. "I want to go back home."

I comforted her as best I could, and explained Amy's situation to DI Myers.

"It's pretty chaotic in there. I can't let her take anything away at the moment but if she lets me have a list of her belongings I'll make sure that they will be available for collection from the station in the next couple of days."

"I'm not sure how much longer we'll be staying in the UK "

"I'll see what I can do. Please make sure you let me know when you and the young lady intend to leave."

Once again we found ourselves kicking our heels at Lewisham Police Station, waiting for a back-up copy of the USB data. Jayne Myers had given us strict instructions not to mention that matter to any other officer in the station which was probably sensible. I was already a familiar face and I recognised several officers – the walrus moustached desk sergeant, for example, and DC Parsons, who had seen me in hospital on the morning after being attacked. He looked surprised to see me again and would have had a word with me had the desk sergeant not called him over.

No way did I feel like making my way back to Barnes on public transport. Uber obliged.

*****

"Help yourself," said Dom, who was half way through a curry when we arrived, "I've made enough for all of us. Though I didn't know if or when you'd be back." He'd regained his usual unflappable composure, and was keen to hear our account of the afternoon's drama

Though Amy, too, was feeling more composed, she excused herself to go to the bathroom, "to freshen up," she said. I guessed she didn't really want to go over those events again.

"How did you know it would be up her fanny?" said Dom, intrigued, after I'd produced the USB copy.

"I couldn't think of any other place where she could be sure it wouldn't be found if the house were searched. It would have been discovered eventually during the post mortem."

My phone trilled. "Jayne Myers here. I am sorry to say that Cassie never regained consciousness. I thought you would like to know that we are now treating Cassie's death as murder. We found no fingerprints on the glass and pill bottle she was supposed to have used. You can pick up Amy's things anytime tomorrow."

I thanked her and said we'd arrange collection. I gave her Howard's home and office numbers but asked that I be allowed to inform him of Cassie's death. It would be of some small consolation for Howard to know that his daughter hadn't taken her own life.

"Brave woman," said Dom, "but so sad."

Amy rejoined us and even managed a faint smile for Dom.

Dom stretched his legs beneath the table and leant back, hands behind his head, while we ate. "By the way, I had a look at your laptop, Ian. That Skype call you thought was from your father. It wasn't from this country. It originated in Australia."

Chapter 15

Monday 5th December : evening

After the traumatic events of the day, I'd been pretty much ready to just crash out. Dom's revelation, however, set my mind in turmoil. My assumptions about my Skype contact had already been shattered, firstly as being from my father and secondly from one of his colleagues. I hadn't yet come up with a viable alternative theory for an unknown caller from the UK and I certainly hadn't even remotely considered that someone in Australia could have been responsible.

We tossed around ideas between the three of us, many highly improbable.

Until Dom said, "Perhaps the intention was firstly to get you out of Sydney and secondly to the UK."

That, I felt, could provide scope for further speculation and investigation.

Dom had further news. "I managed some checking on the other names you gave me," he began, "Christopher Bateman – quite a private individual. No wife or partner of either sex, no Facebook or Twitter presence. He did have a brother, Alexander, but I haven't any further information. He was a lecturer in Art History here in London for many years, and now seems to have a kind of honorary position with the National Portrait Gallery. I can dig further, if you wish."

"That's okay for the moment," I said. "It ties in pretty well with what he told me when we met."

"Now here's the interesting part. Russell Byrne – that's Cassie's older brother – spent two years as a post graduate at the University of London researching art in different cultures. He must have come into contact with

Bateman. And he's very much into social media, where he has at times expressed some fairly strong political views. "

"What about Cassie's ex?" Amy asked.

"Well, he's certainly got a record of political protest. He's Australian by birth, one of three children, but his father emigrated from this country. He's come to the attention of the authorities through jumping on practically every anti-establishment bandwagon since his teens. In the last couple of years he has been linked to white supremacy groups.

Further food for thought. I remembered that I hadn't yet asked Dom's opinion of the scribblings on the notebook page.

"Hmm," he mused. "Not much to go on. The 'co?' could be a question about a website, with 'or' possibly org. The 'wc' before doesn't help – unless you want a website listing all the public loos."

I looked at my watch. Nearly ten o'clock. "Cassie's father should be in his office by now. I ought to tell him what's happened." A task I was not relishing at all.

"Wouldn't it be better to have a look at what Cassie had to say first?" Amy suggested.

"Just a minute," said Dom, and turned the television on. The main new item was the car bomb in Barnes, with the usual guff about following up leads. The police were not treating it as a terrorist threat at present. The newscaster announced that also in the programme was a murder investigation in East London and, with lower priority, coverage of the Prime Minister's visit to Barbados.

Both Amy and I were apprehensive and at the same time intrigued by what Cassie would reveal. Dom plugged the device into his computer.

For Ian and Amy

I am so ashamed of what I have done. I am sure the bad people know that I have already caused the arrest of two members and that I am likely to reveal more information.

I am sure that they will not show me any mercy. It began so innocently. Charlie, my husband, used to take me to rallies where many speakers were very critical of the current political system – and many points made sense. There are things wrong with our system but I soon became opposed to the way Charlie and his followers sought to change it.

Charlie became more extreme and violent in his views, and to me when I disagreed with some of his openly racist comments. I couldn't put up with it and divorced him, though he still tried to contact me. I came to London to get away from him. My brother, Russell, had studied in London for two years under a Dr Bateman, and had become friendly with him. He suggested that I get in touch with Dr Bateman if I needed any help. I didn't know anyone else over here.

He was kind and helpful, particularly when I was finding somewhere to live. He had a friend with a house to let in Lewisham, and said he would get a reduction in the rent if I helped him out with one or two little jobs from time to time. I agreed. I never actually met him.

Nothing happened for a month or so and then he called. He told me someone would visit with a request. The next day I had that call. I was asked to attend some political rallies and take photographs of the speakers and the audience without making my actions obvious. I only met that person once briefly but I have a feeling I've seen him again somewhere – perhaps at the hospital.

I was to send the images to 'wcanhorizon@mail.com' I kept a copy on this memory stick.

Keeping the USB stick in his PC, Dom fired up my laptop, and began searching for the email address.

Amy, I'd already invited you to stay when a couple of weeks ago, I got a phone call from Charlie. He said a journalist from Australia would be visiting Lewisham and a meeting with him would be arranged. He said this journalist was well known for muck raking and publishing damaging articles on fabricated evidence. ...

"Bloody liar!" I exclaimed.

... and he wanted information on what he was doing and where he was going. I told him to go back to Australia, and he just laughed and said he was still there but he knew where I lived and his friends would be paying a visit if I didn't do what I was told. He gave me a mobile number to send the information. I wasn't happy but there didn't seem to be any harm in it so I agreed. I didn't know then that you two would become acquainted.

Ian, I didn't expect to meet you in the A&E department but because I'd been told you weren't a nice person I didn't feel sorry for you. I did pass on that Amy knew where you were staying. I did alert them to the probability you might meet Amy again. I wanted to get Amy away from all the trouble so suggested Brighton. But I also told them that Amy had changed her mind and was going to meet you in Arundel.

When I heard what had happened to Peter Fielder and his wife I was devastated and blamed myself. Knowing also what had happened to your father, Ian, made me even more worried about what I had got involved in. And when they attacked you in my house I had to do something to stop it.

You know the rest.

I am so, so sorry. I want to get out of this mess but if the worst happens please give my love to my parents, and please tell my father that I hold you in no way responsible for my plight.

Cassie Byrne.

We sat in silence not knowing quite what to say. I was glad that Jayne Myers also had this information. Even though it was late I needed to be sure that Byron

Masefield had received the data. I called him on the mobile number he'd given me. He answered almost immediately.

"Byron, it's Ian Fielder. Have you received any information from Jayne Myers of Lewisham Police today?"

"She's been in touch. Why?"

"So you've seen the letter that Cassie Byrne put on a USB stick before she was killed?"

"No, I haven't looked at it yet, though I was told it would be sent over."

"Have you any idea what 'wcanhorizons' is?"

A pause. "Yes"

He seemed disinclined to be more forthcoming without further probing. "Can you tell me?"

A further pause. Longer this time. "Wcan is short for White Canvas."

Well, he wasn't giving much away. I was none the wiser. "Would that be the group my father was investigating by any chance?"

The call was terminated.

"No joy on that email address," said Dom.

I wasn't surprised. "See if you can find out anything about White Canvas. It may well be something with restricted access."

I'd left it long enough to contact Howard. I decided to send an email, with Cassie's letter attached, with a note to contact me urgently on Dom's landline number.

Barely two minutes passed before the phone rang.

"Ian, what the hell's going on? Cassie? Is she all right?"

"Howard," I began in a sombre tone, "I'm sorry to tell you. Cassie died in hospital this evening. She was found alive but unconscious at her house this afternoon with a suspected overdose. It was made to look like suicide but the police are sure she was murdered. The house had been ransacked."

"I ... I want... Ian, how did you find out?" sorrow, anger

or frustration, Howard was having difficulty keeping his voice level.

"Amy and I were due to meet her at a museum. Amy got a text that clearly showed Cassie believed she was in danger. We told the police and went to the house straight away. The police were there by the time we arrived but too late to save her."

"That bastard ... I'll shove his bollocks down his throat..."

I presume he meant Charlie. "I'm not sure her ex-husband was involved."

"Him too!"

Interesting.

"I'll be on the first flight over...."

I interrupted him. "Howard, there's nothing you can do over here. They'll obviously have to do a post mortem, and I presume you would then want her body flown back to Sydney."

"Yes, but ..."

"Hear me out." It wasn't my usual practice to override my boss, but there were things that needed to be said. "Let me make the arrangements here. Then I'm coming back to Sydney as soon as possible. I am convinced that there is a link between London and Sydney regarding the things that I – and my late father -were investigating."

"What else can you tell me?"

"Cassie has given you a lot of the groundwork. I now know that the Skype message that I believed to have come from my father actually came from Australia. Do you have any idea how anyone would have discovered my email address?"

I heard Howard sigh. "That could have been me. I had a call from a Dr Bateman who had been Russell's tutor in London. He apparently was an old friend of your father. Your father was anxious to re-establish contact with you. I was happy to oblige. But that was from London," Howard added thoughtfully.

"You didn't tell me."

"Didn't really think about it. You'd mentioned your father had been in touch. And when you asked for leave to deal with family matters, I assumed that you were going to visit him, or that he was ill."

"He was actually dead. Killed two months ago."

"But ... that's impossible!"

"Apparently not."

Howard had regained composure and made a decision. "Right, you make the arrangements over there. Anyone wants my say- so give them my number, anytime, day or night. I'm going to rattle a few cages over here."

"Will do. I'm planning to fly back tomorrow if possible, so will see you Thursday morning."

Amy was trying to catch my attention. "I want to come with you."

I promised her I'd try to get two seats. To Sydney. She could fly on to Melbourne if she wanted to. I was secretly hoping that she would stay with me a little longer.

Dom had been clacking away on his keyboard. He invited me to look. The screen showed a picture frame surrounding a blank white rectangle. "You're probably right about White Canvas — the access beyond what you see here is strongly password protected.

"Shame, but never mind."

"I didn't say I couldn't gain access but it will take time. I suggest we have a look at the photos on the memory stick. There may be something there we can use."

There must have been about a hundred snapshots not labelled in any way, though the date they were taken was displayed. It would take someone a while to identify where they were taken, now that Cassie couldn't tell us. On a quick flick through I recognised my father in several shots, from the photo his brother had given me. And in one, obviously trying to hide his face, as if he had only just realised he was about to be caught on camera, was Christopher Bateman. No-one else in the photographs rang any bells.

It was getting just past midnight before we were through.

Though Amy had chosen to sleep alone on the first night at Dom's, she took me by the hand and made it clear that her wishes tonight were different. I had no problem with that. Dom raised an eyebrow and grinned as we entered the bedroom.

Despite the restrictions of two adult bodies lying on a bed designed for one, we must have dropped off to sleep very quickly.

Our slumbers were shattered by the sound of breaking glass and much shouting from the street below our window. My watch showed we'd had less than two hours kip.

More hammering on the door and my phone ringing. I looked out of the window as I pressed the answer button. There were police everywhere, some armed.

"Ian, this is Byron. Can you please come down?"

I pulled on my jeans and a thick pullover. "Wait here!" I said to Amy.

Broken glass from a smashed door panel lay strewn on the mat. I brushed it aside with the heel of my trainers and opened the door. Byron Masefield and Jayne Myers stood there. Beyond, in the street, two handcuffed men were being led to squad cars.

"May we come in?" asked Byron.

I led them upstairs. Dom stood there in a tatty dressing gown, bleary eyed. I introduced him

Byron began, "We have just arrested four people on suspicion of aggravated burglary."

"Four?"

"We have had this house under surveillance since you returned. Inspector Myers suspected that there would be an attempt on your life."

"But how did they know the address?"

"I'm afraid I used you to set a trap," said Jayne Myers. "To test whether you were right in suspecting someone at the police station to be passing information. I purposely left your address on my office desk – and someone took the bait. Detective Constable Parsons is now in a cell and his home is being searched."

"We are keeping a very close watch on Christopher Bateman," said Byron, "but we haven't got a shred of direct evidence to hold him or even to request a search warrant." He paused. "I'm hoping that you may be able to help us."

"I've already booked a flight back to Sydney tomorrow – sorry, this evening. For both of us."

"This shouldn't take long," he said.

"Look, we need to collect Amy's stuff from Lewisham Police Station, and no doubt you'll both want to take further statements. We also need to sort out some arrangements for getting Cassie's body back to Sydney ..."

Jayne Myers interrupted "No problem, Mr Fielder. I will arrange for Amy's stuff to be brought here. You can refer the Australian Embassy, undertakers or whatever, to me to make arrangements for Cassie, and as long as I have your email, phone and contact address in Sydney I don't see any need to prolong your stay in this country."

"So what is it you want me to do?" I said, resigned to give the assistance they needed.

"We want you to visit Christopher Bateman again. On your own. If he is involved he would regard you as presenting a potential threat to his anonymity in these events. However, we believe he has no reason to suspect that you have found any incriminating link to him."

"What do you want me to say?"

"Something innocuous. Thank him for his help, ask him to keep in touch, look you up if he comes to Australia.

That kind of thing."

"And what do you expect him to do?"

"Unless he's innocent he won't throw away an opportunity to remove the threat you pose to him once and for all."

"In other words, you expect him to kill me."

"We will be on hand. You will be wired, and will wear a vest."

"Okay," I agreed. Though I was scared shitless.

Chapter 16

Tuesday 6ᵗʰ December

I'd set my alarm for 8 am but in truth I hadn't slept much after the intrusion. My mind was in full speculative mode of everything that could go wrong at my meeting with Bateman. Amy might have two body bags to take back home.

We agreed over breakfast that Amy should pay a call to the Australian High Commission in the Strand to seek advice on the repatriation of the murder victim of one of their citizens, and provide them with the necessary contact information. I hoped to join her after lunch but that might depend on how things panned out. Otherwise we'd meet back at Dom's at teatime. I privately asked Dom to make sure she got the flight regardless of what happened to me.

Christopher Bateman had taken my call and if he was surprised, he had concealed it well.

"Why, of course, Ian, I'm so glad you thought of me before flying home. You're lucky, I don't have to be at the gallery until after lunch."

The simplest way by rail from Barnes to Morden was via Clapham Junction, where I was taken into the transport police office and fitted up with the necessary equipment. I took another local train to Malden South. It was then a short walk along Martin's Way to Bateman's house, off Links Avenue. I looked around for evidence of a police presence but could see none. But if I couldn't see them, neither would Bateman. Nevertheless, I was apprehensive, to say the least.

"Come in, come in, Ian. Come and sit down." He was dressed more formally than previously, in a three-piece dark grey suit. "Would you like to take your coat off?"

"No, it's okay, thanks. I can't stay long. Quite a few things to do before I leave. I just wanted to call and say thank you."

"I haven't done much," he said

"Well, you were able to tell me a lot more about my father than I knew before."

"So you are returning to Australia? I take it you have satisfactorily concluded all your business here?"

"One or two loose ends still. I was shocked to discover that my editor's daughter was murdered here in London yesterday. I'm helping to arrange repatriation of the body."

Christopher frowned briefly. "I'm sorry to hear that. Do they know who did it?"

"They are pursuing enquiries," I said.

"Excuse me a moment," he said. He went into the kitchen. I could hear him talking to someone on the phone."

His attitude had changed when he came back. "You know, Ian, much though I respect your talents as an investigative journalist, you have caused me no end of problems."

"What do you mean?"

"Your father was getting uncomfortably close to finding out about White Canvas. That's my pet project to put this country back on the proper track. When I learned from my contacts overseas that his son had begun similar investigations shortly after John's … ah … unfortunate accident, I put two and two together …"

"And made five. I never had any contact with my father."

"I'm inclined to believe you now. But I was convinced that your father had passed on some damaging information. I agreed to the deception to get you to England where we could find out what you knew and at the same time stop you interfering in Australia. You won't be going back there."

"Why did you have to involve Cassie?"

"Ah, yes, that poor young lass."

"Save the crocodile tears!" I snapped.

"She was merely a back-up. Unfortunately when you were hospitalised we had to use her. You were supposed to have been brought in for interrogation but that moron tried to kill you."

"The dead body?"

He nodded. "But then you were free to investigate. I underestimated you. Even my contact at the police station lost you for a while. I gather he's been arrested but I expect you knew that."

"Late last night. Did he kill Cassie?" She may well have known that Parsons was a detective. She would have let him in her house without question. I recalled her last frantic text message *'He's here. Police...'* Was that a request for us to call the police or that she'd recognised her caller as a policeman?

"You will have to ask him."

I'm sure Jayne Myers would be doing just that.

"You were very clever to trace me through an unfortunate reference to John's nickname. It was Peter who mentioned it, I presume?"

"Yes."

"In what context, may I ask?"

"There were others at your school who knew of nicknames. One of them was at the funeral and mentioned them to Peter."

"That was a most unfortunate slip of the tongue." Bateman was deep in thought, probably trying to remember former classmates and figure out which one was responsible – and what action to take. He spoke again. "I wanted to know what other information Peter Fielder may have passed on to you or would pass on to anyone else. I couldn't take the risk. But by the time I found out, the cat was already out of the bag. Most regrettable."

I didn't know whether he was referring to the torching of Peter's house and Elsie's death or the slip of the tongue.

I decided to up the ante. "When we met before you implied that you knew of my father's death. Yet you had been out of contact with him, and his death was never reported in the newspaper."

"Is that so? Oh well, old comrades, grapevine, you know."

Bloody hypocrite.

"And now, Ian, I regret that I'm going to arrange for you to meet your father. You can write all about me in the Gospel News." He pulled a handgun from his pocket.

"I still don't understand what this all has to do with your White Canvas project or whatever you call it."

"Really? You disappoint me." His lips curled. "We have this jumped up black poofter telling us how to run the country and half his bloody cabinet are every shade of brown. White Canvas will start again and put Britain back where it should be."

"In the dark ages ..."

"Shut up, that's enough," he spat at me, and started to raise his gun.

"Armed police! Drop your weapon!" came the cry as armed officers burst in through both doors. One pushed me aside out of the line of fire.

Initial surprise showed on Bateman's face then he smiled and put the gun into his mouth. And fired.

Byron gave me a helping hand off the floor,. "You okay?"

"Left it a bit late didn't you?"

He shrugged, "We wanted to get everything on tape. If you hadn't asked that last question we would have been in sooner."

My bloody fault then if I'd copped it. But Bateman's answer set off some alarm bells in my mind. "Do you know how long the Prime Minister's Commonwealth tour has been planned?"

"He mentioned the idea soon after he entered Downing Street. The itinerary has probably been in place for two or three months." He looked at me thoughtfully. "I can see where you are going with this. It has been on our mind too but we've had very little to go on, only speculation."

"Is his schedule well known?"

"Why, yes. Details of his visits are on the internet."

Byron had thanked me for my role in exposing Christopher Bateman, and assured me that Special Branch would be in touch with their Australian counterparts.

*****

Amy had just finished her business with the Australian High Commission when I called her to assure her that I was safe and well, and also free of other commitments for the rest of the day.

"I'll meet you by the London Eye," I said. "It's just across the river from where you are now. You can't miss it! I'll get the tube to Waterloo from Morden. See you in about half an hour."

Although there were still some unanswered questions which I hoped to resolve when I got back home, I felt as if I could relax for the first time since I'd arrived in London a week ago. Even the weather was being kind – crisp and cold as one would expect for the time of year but bright and sunny.

Amy was waiting for me with a huge hug and a kiss.

"All sorted?" I said.

"Pretty much so. They will need her father's

authorisation but they will liaise with the police and the coroner's office."

We found a convenient cafe nearby, and I recounted the events of the morning to her while we ate. A look of horror passed over her face when she heard how close I'd come to being shot. She took my hand and said softly, "I didn't want to lose you."

"You've had a pretty shitty time since you've been here for what was supposed to be a holiday, and you've seen very little of London, let alone anywhere else. How about we make use of our last afternoon here with some sightseeing along by the river?"

"I'd like that, Ian."

My phone warbled. My heart sank when I looked at the caller display. I didn't really want to spend another afternoon at Lewisham Police Station. Reluctantly, I answered.

"Jayne Myers here. Just thought you'd like to know that we've found records of phone calls linking Detective Constable Parsons to Cassie Byrne and to Dr Bateman, and some emails to a Charles Saunders, who I believe is Cassie's former husband. We think Parsons may be responsible for her murder. Quite a lot of pamphlets too stashed away from UKIP and other organisations even further to the right."

"You don't want me to come to the station again?"

"That won't be necessary. And I've had Miss Cadwallader's belongings sent over to your friend's address in Barnes

"Thank you very much."

I told Amy the good news. Jayne Myer's report had, however, raised a question.

"Tell me, how well did you know Cassie's husband?"

"Not very well. As I told you before, I didn't really like him. He was big mates with Russ – that's Cassie's brother – and my brother, Steve. They were all in the same class at school.

I needed to tread carefully. "Does he still hang out with Charlie?"

"Not these days, I think. Steve was always full of ideas and energy, quite a hothead at one time and shared some common views with Charlie and Russ. But ever since he left university he's directed his energy much more positively.

"In what way?"

"He's working for a charity that helps children in the third world countries."

Hardly consistent with extreme right wing political activity.

"What about Russell?"

"I don't know. You can ask him when we get back home." She picked up a sense of where the conversation might be heading. "You surely don't suspect either of them of being involved?"

"Not directly, I'm sure." I hope I sounded convincing. "However, Russ may have unwittingly established a link between Bateman and Charlie. He would have got to know Bateman quite well through the university."

"Mmm. You're not going to get him in trouble are you?"

"No. I just wondered if he could give me any handle on Charlie Saunders."

Amy seemed to accept my explanation, and I had no desire to spoil her – our – last afternoon in London by pressing the matter any further.

We walked along the river past the National Theatre and the Globe, had a nose around Borough Market and Southwark Cathedral before heading over London Bridge.

"That's amazing. So different to Melbourne or Sydney," said Amy.

I agreed. Despite having lived and worked in London I preferred the latter. "What else would you like to see?"

"Well, I suppose I ought to at least see Buckingham Palace."

"Okay, we'll get the tube to Westminster and walk from there."

We strolled arm in arm along Birdcage Walk to the Palace. I waved in the general direction of Downing Street. "That's where the Prime Minister hangs out when he's not gallivanting around the world."

We still had time to wander further on to Hyde Park, at least far enough to see the Serpentine. Amy was beginning to flag and the lack of sleep we'd had in the last disturbed night was catching up on both of us. If we headed back to Barnes now we would miss the rush hour. The credit left on my Oyster card was just enough to cover the train from Victoria. Amy had bought a day's Travelcard.

I rang Dom and told him to hold off getting any dinner. I felt it was the least we could do to treat him to a proper meal at a restaurant for all the impositions I'd made on his time and hospitality over the previous week. His computer skills had also helped me get answers – or most of them – to the questions that had brought me to London. He had one last piece of information for me.

"I managed to get inside that White Canvas site or rather peek through the door. You'd need to go on the dark web to get to its inner sanctums."

"Meaning what?"

"It's, like, an underground network that only people with the right connections can access, Most of the extreme porn is on the dark web."

"So what were you able to find?"

"It's definitely a right-wing clandestine organisation intent on bringing about political change, not just here in the UK but elsewhere. They are not averse to using violence to achieve their aims. It seems to work on a cell structure and I get the impression that access to the site is limited to a small number of individuals in each country. Each group, or possibly country, is identified by an Alpha, Bravo, Charlie code. So you may be looking for an Alpha male in Australia!"

"Well that gives me something to work on."

When it came to our final farewell as the taxi arrived to take us to Heathrow, Amy put her arms round Dom. "Thank you so much," she said, and planted the biggest kiss ever on his lips.

I'd never seem Dom blush before.

"Take care," I said, "and I hope that you will come and visit us before too long."

We arrived at Heathrow in good time to check in with Singapore Airlines and relax in the departure lounge. While Amy was browsing the shops I fired up my laptop to check on the details of the Prime Minister's world tour.

Canada he'd already done, he would shortly be leaving Barbados – his father's homeland, apparently – and then on to Canberra, arriving on Thursday morning at much the same time as we'd be touching down in Sydney. Then next Monday morning he would be flying on to Wellington, and thence homeward with three stopovers en route in Singapore, Pretoria, and Delhi, it seemed pretty straightforward, though there was something I couldn't identify nagging in my mind.

Chapter 17

Wednesday 7th into Thursday 8th December

On the long haul to Singapore, once the late meal had been served and even before the lights dimmed, we both crashed out completely for, what, nine or ten hours unbroken sleep. I don't think we would have noticed if a brass band had been playing full blast in the cabin. We had a couple of hours stopover at Changi. Enough to stretch our legs, freshen up and grab a coffee, before the final stage to Sydney.

We both wanted to get more sleep. Amy managed more catnapping than I. It wasn't helped by the turbulence as we flew over the long chain of the Philippines, with the result that the serving of the first meal – supper, midnight feast or whatever – was delayed by nearly half an hour.

The niggling matter that had plagued me before we'd left London came to my mind again, in the form of a question. If the PM was arriving in Canberra on Thursday (Was it Thursday already, I wondered?) and not leaving for New Zealand until the following Monday, what was he doing on the days in between? His schedule hadn't specified. In all other countries it was literally barely more than a flying visit, with just enough time for formal meetings with the appropriate Head of State.

I must have eventually dropped off again. When I woke up, I could see that dawn was beginning to break and the stewards were preparing to serve breakfast.

"Good morning, sleepyhead," said Amy, straining against her seat belt to kiss me. She seemed as bright as a daisy.

All in all, I didn't feel too bad myself.

Over breakfast, I raised a point which we hadn't talked about previously. "Amy, what are your plans when we get to Sydney?"

She was taking some time to consider her reply.

"You are welcome to stay with me, or perhaps you will want to see your family in Melbourne."

"I've been trying to decide," she said. "I dread the thought of not seeing you again, Ian, but I think really I ought to go home first." She looked at me. "We will keep in touch, won't we?"

"Absolutely." I replied. "If not before, then we will both be at Cassie's funeral."

"Yes, indeed," she said, a smile breaking into her previously solemn expression.

Even so, we still were reluctant to say goodbye after we'd gone through customs and she prepared to head off to the domestic terminal at Kingsford Smith for a connecting flight to Melbourne.

Waiting to meet me in the arrivals hall was my boss, Howard Byrne. A tall, middle aged, slightly balding gent in a well-pressed suit stood beside him.

"Howard, I'm so sorry about Cassie ..."

"Don't blame yourself, Ian, it wasn't your fault." His eyes looked bloodshot, and his voice was uncharacteristically subdued. "Ian, this is Inspector Stan Ellison. He's with the Federal Police."

I took his offered hand.

"Our colleagues from London have been in touch about a possible attempt on the life of your Prime Minister, who..." he looked at his watch, "... should be arriving in Canberra very soon. Obviously we have stepped up the security measures. Is there anything that you can add?"

"Not really. I presume you have been given the name of Charlie Saunders, who may well be involved?"

"We have. He's not been seen at his Canberra address

for a couple of weeks. We are actively searching for him."

"It seems likely that he, or some of his colleagues, set up a scam to get me to England. I was investigating activities of the far right here in Australia and it's possible I was getting close to a breakthrough. There is certainly evidence of links to a clandestine far right group in the UK that hopefully has now been exposed and closed down."

"Very well. If you think of anything else, please give me a call." He handed me a card.

Howard offered me a lift. "I've got my car outside. I'll drive you home and you can bring me up to speed on the way. I presume you didn't drive to the airport?"

"That's right."

"Oh by the way, I thought Amy would be with you."

"We travelled back together. She's going home to Melbourne. But we will be keeping in touch."

I wanted confirmation. "It was you, I presume, who arranged for her to be sitting next to me on the flight to Heathrow?"

"Yes, it was. She was on her own, travelling to a country the other side of the world. You were on your own, on family business I supposed. It seemed a good idea at the time. I didn't foresee that you were both going to get mixed up in funny business involving Cassie."

"In Cassie's last letter – which you have seen – she mentions your son, Russell."

"What of it?"

"I'd like to meet him. There are one or two things that he may be able to help me with."

Silence, then, "We're not talking."

Delicate subject. I guess that Howard was holding him in some way responsible for his sister's fate.

"Okay. Can you give me a phone number or address where I can contact him? Is he here in Sydney?"

"Probably." He thought for a moment. "Look, if you do talk to him, I'd appreciate it if you could let me know of anything … ah … important. And I don't want you to involve the police."

He sighed. "We parted on rather bad terms."

Probably because Howard had given Russell a right bollocking, as I recalled his comments to me over the phone a couple of nights ago.

At that time in the morning, traffic was still light, and we were soon at the small flat I rented in the suburb of Ashfield. We didn't need to go through the centre of Sydney.

"Plans for the rest of the day?"

"I don't know. Crash out. Gather my thoughts. Then back to work I suppose."

"You can take a few more days leave, if you want."

"I'd just be twiddling my thumbs," I said. In truth I felt rather deflated. After days of action I was back home with nothing really to occupy my attention. Except… "Howard, one thing that has been puzzling me. Peel-Jackson's schedule. He's arrived in Canberra today but he's not flying to New Zealand until Monday. What's he doing on Friday, Saturday and Sunday?"

"I really don't know. Downtime with his wife? Recovering from jet lag?"

"I wasn't aware that his wife was accompanying him."

"Oh probably, but low profile. Anyhow, I can find out his plans and email you."

I said goodbye, went inside and flopped out in the armchair gazing at the blank wall. Empty house, sour milk and stale food in the fridge and I hadn't stocked up with beer. I switched the TV on. The Prime Minister had arrived safely, and was likely to be in formal and exclusive company for the rest of the day.

I sent Amy a text, 'All ok? Ring whenever.'

I glanced at the phone images I'd taken of my father's notebook page. The scribblings still seemed gobbledegook.

CsB? CS
wc co? or (page torn)
(page torn) PJ
(page torn) 0 ? x
128Cb?
1210S/Pm?
125 x 1212Bb

Before I made myself too comfortable I decided to take a walk to the nearby mall to get some food from Aldi or Woolworth's, and call in the bottle shop as well. All the way there and back my mind was turning over the events of the past twelve days, which raised a worrying thought. While key people in the apparent White Canvas movement had probably been removed from the scene in London, there was a distinct possibility that those conspirators in Sydney would have been made aware of my return. Rather than being out of personal danger I realised I might still be at risk.

Although most of the information I had previously gathered from my investigations was stored on my laptop, which I had taken with me to London, I decided to check the folder of notes I had made on the off-chance that I might find some further clue to the White Canvas connection in Australia.

The folder was missing from my desk drawer, along with the back-up USB stick. I realised that some other items on my desk were not as I had left them. Someone had taken great care to make the search of my flat as unobtrusive as possible.

I might not have discovered anything was missing for some time.

My mobile warbled, interrupting my thoughts as to what I should do about the burglary. There was a text message from Howard.

PM in Sydney Saturday, Brisbane Sunday. Low key

private visits, doing the tourist thing. Wants to see Botany Bay, Government House, Opera House, Great Barrier Reef.

He could have seen all of Botany Bay just by looking out of the window of his jet on the approach to Kingsford Smith, oil terminals and all. Perhaps he was expecting to see the remains of the transport ships and the ghosts of shackled prisoners. Almost every TV footage of Sydney would show the iconic Opera House. True, it was equally impressive close up in real life but worth a special journey? His choice I suppose. And the Great Barrier Reef? He wasn't going to see much of that this side of Brisbane.

The Government House on his schedule was interesting. I assumed he had in mind the residence of several former governors of New South Wales in the first half of the nineteenth century when the richer Parramatta, to the west, was the seat of government rather than the more dismal dock area that was Sydney at the time. The house was now in the hands of the Australian equivalent of the National Trust.

I looked at the images from the notebook page again. Cb – Canberra ? Pm Parramatta? Bb – Brisbane? Tenuous and unsubstantiated extrapolation ? Probably. The numbers I couldn't explain – unless, perhaps they represented the date 128 Cb – 8th December Canberra. Today. Which would make 10th December Parramatta and 12th December Brisbane. The other number for Brisbane would have been 5th December when he was still in ... I thought back to the Ten O' Clock News at Dom's ... Barbados! Still speculation. If I was wrong well, okay, I'd look foolish. I could live with that. I couldn't live with the thought that inaction on my part might have fatal consequences.

I fished out the card I'd been given and called Stan Ellison. He answered almost immediately.

"It's Ian Fielder here. I've been looking at an image I took of my father's notebook. I might have found a connection." I explained my speculation quite expecting him to dismiss them out of hand.

On the contrary he took them very seriously. "That's very interesting. There is an informal visit planned to Government House on Saturday. I think we can dismiss any threat at Canberra. There was no sign of any trouble before he disappeared behind closed doors for the rest of day."

"There is one other thing," I said. "While I was in the UK, someone got into my flat and took my back-up notes on my investigations."

"Anything else taken? Any sign of forced entry?"

"No."

"Have you been aware on anyone following you or watching your flat?"

"Not at all, but as you know I only returned a few hours ago."

"Ian, I think in the circumstances, and for your own safety it would be unwise to stay in your flat, certainly for the next couple of days. Can you stay with a friend?"

I was reluctant to put any of my friends in Sydney in danger. "I'll find a hotel," I replied.

I had a further idea. "Look, I know it may be expecting a lot, but as you know, I am a journalist. I would very much appreciate the opportunity of being present at the PM's visit there. In the background, if you like."

Stan hesitated before replying "I think we could arrange that. With the proviso that we have a preview of anything you write about it, and the power of veto."

They could probably veto it without my agreement anyway. "Okay," I said.

"Don't tell anyone else about this. Let me know where you re staying and I'll be in touch."

Chapter 18

Friday 9th December

Surprisingly,I had a pretty good and dreamless sleep for most of the night. Until I woke up at 5 am in a strange bed. I'd followed Stan's advice and taken b&b at Ashfield Manor Hotel. My mind started racing, trying to untangle the several loose threads of the past weeks from the Gordian Knot of speculation.

Whatever role Charlie Saunders was playing in this business, it was a sure bet that he wasn't working alone. Were his siblings involved? I still didn't have a direct connection between him and Christopher Bateman. Not so for Russell Byrne. He might be a completely blameless bystander or into it up to his neck. I wasn't confident that I would get any answers even if I did get to speak to him.

The Skype connection again came into my mind. I remembered hearing a rumbling train that had seemed in keeping with the supposed location in Lewisham. But if the location was in Australia then it also had to be near a railway, unless I had imagined the sound. Dom hadn't told me where in Australia.

Barely 6 am. But 7 pm in the evening in the UK. Quicker to ring Dom than fire up my laptop. He answered immediately.

"Hi, Dom. Yes I'm back home, thanks," I replied to his query. "A question: were you able to narrow down the location of the Skyping other than somewhere in Australia?"

"Er, yes, but I didn't write it down and you didn't ask. I'm pretty certain it was Melbourne … but it might have been Sydney or Canberra. Definitely one of those."

Only three large cities then to search!

"By the way," he continued, "I was going to email you. I looked at that White Canvas website again. It would be a darn sight easier to get into the Pentagon files than crack the security they've set up, so can't really give you any more info on that."

I hoped Dom hadn't actually tried hacking into the Pentagon. I thanked him and rang off, promising to keep in touch. Was his information actually any help? Debatable.

I had a bizarre thought. There was a Railway Terrace in Sydney's Lewisham, a couple of suburbs towards the city centre from Ashfield. The imposters would have to have been really cocky and confident that their deception would not be discovered to set up the Skype connection in a parallel address. I tried to dismiss it as just one coincidence too many. Nevertheless when I powered up my laptop I couldn't resist checking to see whether Melbourne also had a Railway Terrace. Surprisingly, it did, though not in a Lewisham suburb.

Over breakfast I was still tossing around the idea of investigating the tenuous and unlikely link but I couldn't see anything to be gained by it. The perpetrators, if they'd got even a smidgeon of common sense, would be long gone anyhow. The Skype was still a niggling loose end, no matter.

I was expecting a call back from Stan Ellison. I grabbed my phone immediately it rang. It wasn't Stan.

"Is that Ian? Hi, it's Steve, Amy's brother here. She said you might like to talk to me. About Charlie Saunders?"

"Yes, indeed. Thanks very much for contacting me."

"What is it you want to know?"

"Are you still in regular contact with him?"

"Not really. We were mates at school, but rather went our own ways after that and I've only seen him occasionally since. I believe he is working in Canberra now."

"So you don't know much about his political views?"

"Oh yes, he never made any secret about those! Even at school he was pretty forthright about the place of anyone who didn't have a white skin. In recent years he seems to have moved further to the right than Hitler. Runs in the family, so I've heard."

"You don't share his views?"

"We tagged along with him for a while, but as I said, when I went to university we lost touch. I don't support his politics in any way."

"You said 'we' tagged along? Who else would that be?"

"Sorry, I assumed you knew. Russ Byrne. He and Charlie still remained good friends I believe even after his sister's divorce. I gather from Russ that Charlie wasn't too chuffed about you probing into far-right groups."

"Any idea how he would have known about that in the first place?"

"Probably from Russ, though you may have triggered some alarm bells yourself."

"It sounds as if you are still friendly with Russ. Would you know if he has similar views to Charlie?"

"Difficult to say. He's not so open with his opinions on politics but, let me say, it would not surprise me if he has right-wing leanings, even if not as extreme as Charlie's."

"How is he taking the death of his sister?"

"Not well. Two nights ago I bumped into him in a bar we often frequent. Three quarters pissed, drowning his sorrows. From what little sense I could make of his slurred utterings, it seems his father holds him responsible for what happened to Cassie. Maybe he also shares some guilt."

"Do you think he'd talk to me?"

"At the moment I guess he doesn't want to talk to anybody."

"Okay, no worries. Tell me, have you ever heard of White Canvas? Perhaps from Charlie or Russ?"

"No. What is it?"

"It doesn't matter. Anyhow, give my thanks to Amy for asking you to call. Tell her I'll be in touch soon."

The rest of Friday passed uneventfully. No flash of enlightenment resulted from a rather pointless trip I made two stations up the line to walk along the length of Railway Terrace. I tried picking up the threads of my investigation before I'd left for London, but without much enthusiasm or sense of purpose. Perhaps I was even losing the thread.

Despite Steve's comments I tried the cell phone number for Russell Byrne that Howard had reluctantly given me but just got the answerphone. I left a message to ring me back.

Time even seemed to stand still after I got a call from Stan Ellison late in the afternoon to say that a car would pick me up at 9.30 on Saturday morning. I let him know where I was staying. He rang off before I could ask any further questions.

Chapter 19

Saturday 10th December

It was, in fact, Stan himself who came for me. We sat in the back while his driver headed towards Parramatta, taking the M4 toll road. He briefed me on the set up. "We have some other information which taken in conjunction with your theory leads us to believe that there is a real threat centred around the Government House visit. It has been closed to the public, though in fact that closure was already in place, and only key staff will be on site during the visit, namely the Director of the National Trust, his on-site manager and an experienced guide. Apart from police, no other vehicles will be permitted in the park area, and the Prime Minister will arrive by helicopter. The place was also closed yesterday when we carried out a thorough search of the premises for any hidden explosive devices. It has remained under surveillance since. You will stay in the car about one hundred yards from the entrance until the Prime Minister and his party have entered and then you may approach the entrance but please stay outside the gate. Any questions?"

"I don't think so."

Almost as a casual afterthought he added, "By the way, we picked up someone trying to gain entry to your flat last night. We've had it under surveillance."

Christ! Thinking back to what happened at Dom's I had another concern, "Would you arrange for someone to check over my car? Someone tried to blow me up in London after the hire car I was using was fitted with a tracking device."

"Hmm, yes, that would be wise," he said

We entered the park area and pulled up, thankfully under the shade of a tree, short of the entrance to

Government House and its cafe, as the sign advertised. There were three other unmarked cars along that same stretch and three more on the other side of the park.

We waited for about ten minutes until the chop-chop of an approaching helicopter could be heard. Stan and his driver got out of the car. Stan had his hand on his gun. As soon as the helicopter had landed and the rotors stopped, three armed men clambered out and formed a protective cordon around the V.I.P. as he emerged into the morning sun. Despite the rapidly rising temperature, he wore a light grey coat and a trilby pulled down almost over his eyes. The group walked briskly towards the entrance. Stan and other plains clothes officers were scanning the whole of the location for signs of anything untoward.

As they entered the gate, I got out of the car and walked towards the entrance. Inside, a well-dressed and upright gentleman, presumably the Trust Director, came out of the reception office to welcome his distinguished visitor. Behind him a middle-aged woman in a smart trouser suit emerged, looking, I thought, distinctly unhappy. She was followed closely by a young fair haired man wearing a jacket with the Trust logo and an identity tag hanging from a lanyard around his neck. His left hand was in his jacket pocket, his right hand ready to shake that of the visitor.

In an instant, as the young man got closer, he drew a pistol and shot the Prime Minister at point blank range.

I saw the look of surprise on his face as he realised he'd shot the wrong man. He sprinted the short distance towards the exit, as I dropped back behind the gate. The police, although taken by surprise and instinctively trying to catch the victim as he fell, recovered quickly but had no clear line of sight to fire before he was hidden by the gate.

I was closest to him. Without thought I gave chase, though I could hear Stan yelling, "Get out of the way you stupid bugger!" as he also gave pursuit.

The attacker still had his gun but to turn and fire he

would lose ground and even if he took me down he would not escape the weapons trained on him by the posse. He was heading down towards the river, the slope becoming steeper. He stumbled slightly, enough for me to launch a flying tackle and bring him down. He was quickly surrounded by police and cuffed.

Stan hauled me to my feet, "You stupid twat, you could have been killed!"

I dusted myself down. "But you've got your man. Alive, for questioning."

"Yes," he conceded. "You did well."

As the perpetrator was led away to a police car, and we walked back to the gate, I heard the sirens of an ambulance.

"The Prime Minister ... is he ..."

"He's safe," said Stan, "We used a decoy. He'll have some nasty bruising but his heavy duty Kevlar vest will have saved him from serious harm."

The Director was sitting on a chair at the cafe, head in his hands, looking shell-shocked. The police were interviewing the distraught manageress.

"That young man should not have been here today. He's only been with us for a few weeks, though I must say his work has been exemplary. He arrived late, and told me that Clive, our senior guide, had been taken ill this morning and had asked him to stand in at short notice. Clive should have rung me. It was too late for me to do anything about it. And your officer let him in."

I reckoned the officer in question was going to get an earful.

"He did have the right credentials, madam." said Stan. "Have you got Clive's address? We need to check."

Stan turned to me. "You are not to make public any of the details of what's happened here this morning. We will be making a press statement to say that a man was detained for questioning on suspicious activity."

I started to protest.

"Write a novel instead! And you can report on the Prime Minister's actual visit. We have given him the all clear. He'll be arriving soon."

*****

The evening paper gave a report of the Prime Minister's visit to Government House, with a bit of the history of the building. Buried on an inside page was a small paragraph to say that a Mr Robert Saunders had been arrested for causing an affray with the intent of endangering life. I presumed he was Charlie's brother. I realised that although I'd heard a lot about him, I'd never actually seen a photo of Charlie.

A couple of days later, I had a courtesy call from Stan Ellison. He apologised for being short with me at Parramatta, and thanked me for my help in averting a major diplomatic crisis and bringing the sick bastard (his words) to justice. The senior guide had been found tied up and gagged at his home. A laptop had been seized during the search of the flat Robert Saunders was renting under an assumed name. His phone had revealed recent exchanges with Charlie, who had also been arrested along with a couple of other activists. Stan reported also that no devices had been found on my car, and he thought it would be safe for me to return to my flat.

I felt it appropriate to make a request. "I would be very grateful if you could provide me with any information that could help me complete my intended magazine article on far right activists in Australia. Obviously I wouldn't expect anything for publication which would prejudice a forthcoming trial."

He didn't reject the idea out of hand. "I'll see what we can do. There is a story to be told to the general public I believe."

Chapter 19

One month later

With the Christmas and New Year holidays in the UK and in Australia, it was early January before Cassie's body was eventually released and repatriated.

In the meantime, Stan Ellison had given me some information and follow-up leads which had proved invaluable in getting my feature article ready for publication. In particular he told me that they were confident that whatever designs White Canvas had planned to establish a new white supremacy regime had been well and truly scuppered both in the UK and in Australia. The Alpha male Dom had jokingly referred to wasn't one of the Saunders clan but a British immigrant, Alex Pearson, formerly known as Alexander Bateman.

I'd been in contact with Uncle Peter. I had found out from the hospital that he had been discharged and was staying with a friend. He was still weak after his ordeal, but surprisingly philosophical about his future. He'd said that he might even visit me in Sydney, and I had assured him he would be most welcome.

I had, of course, also kept in touch with Amy, and I had accepted an invitation to spend New Year with her and her family. She had come up from Melbourne to stay with me for Cassie's funeral. Amy's brother, though invited, had declined due to other commitments.

Though Howard was originally from that city he had been working in Sydney for several years, ever since his children had flown the nest, so to speak. I'd visited his home for drinks on one occasion just after I'd been taken on by his publishing house , 'to get to know each other', as he'd said. His house, or rather, a large single storey bungalow, sat in an elevated position in the northern suburb of Watson, and enjoyed an impressive view of the whole expanse of Sydney harbour, with the famous bridge and the few city centre skyscrapers just visible in the distance.

He'd lost his wife to cancer only last year. She was buried in the nearby South Head Cemetery, which was to be his daughter's resting place too, next to her mother.

The small church was packed, with family – aunts, uncles and cousins, I supposed – and friends. Former colleagues too, probably. Amy pointed out that she'd thought one young woman in the congregation had been working in the hospital at Lewisham. Amy and I stood together a few rows from the front in the church of St Peter's as Howard and his son Russell followed the coffin up the aisle.

Russell had never returned my call. I'd wondered whether he did feel any responsibility for his sister's death. He had introduced her to Bateman, he was a friend of Saunders, and, according to Steve, he probably still held right-wing views as he had in the past. He had, as far as I knew, not been approached by the police after the shooting, so presumably they had found no link to him among Saunders' contacts. Howard had received Cassie's account in full, and the resulting issues he'd had with his son must have been resolved. Otherwise they would not be walking side by side behind Cassie's coffin. It didn't seem my place to poke a stick into a hornet's nest on this stressful family occasion, or subsequently.

At the appropriate point during the service, Howard stood to make an address.

"Thank you all for coming here today to pay tribute to my lovely daughter whose life was taken so tragically. She had everything to live for, thankfully having been released from an unfortunate marriage. However, I cannot in my heart forgive her ex-husband for his part in her death, even if indirectly." His voice began to falter, but he continued, "Nevertheless, I am sure Cassie would have wanted you to remember her in times of happiness and joy and friendship, to pay your respects but to go beyond grieving for her and enjoy your own lives."

He dabbed his eyes with a handkerchief.

"After this service, her body will be taken to South Head for burial, and I would ask only family members to attend. I would like to invite you all to meet in the church hall here for refreshments. I will join you shortly."

Amy too was wiping tears from her face.

After the final hymn and prayers, we made our way out into the sunshine, and followed other mourners to the hall nearby. An extensive buffet covered the tables down the centre of the hall and wine, soft drinks and tea were being served at the end. Out of respect, we held back from filling our plates until Howard and his relatives returned. Around the side of the room were a multitude of photographs of Cassie from childhood through to young adult.

"Such a sad day," said Amy, "but so beautiful here," as she took in the vista over the waters.

"Fancy living here?" I said, but not with any seriousness.

"Doubt if I could afford it, but, Ian, I've been meaning to tell you. I applied for a job in the University Library in Sydney. I've just heard I've been accepted."

I was gobsmacked. "Congratulations, Amy." I gave her a hug and a kiss. "You'll be looking for somewhere to stay?"

She nodded.

"I'd be happy for you to share my place."

Gosh, she had a lovely smile.

The arrival of Howard soon led to a gathering round the food tables. Amy and I helped ourselves generously and wandered over to look at the photographs. Amy would obviously have recognised Cassie from her earlier years. I was quite surprised, given Howard's comments in church, that a couple of Cassie's wedding photos were on display. Though of course, that would have been a happy occasion, I assumed. The young man who was obviously the groom, Charlie, was stocky, bearded and with long hair tied at the back in a pony tail. The man just behind him was also bearded. I looked again closely at the photograph.

"Amy," I said. "You were at Cassie's wedding, I guess. Do you know the person standing behind Charlie?"

"That's Charlie's father," she said.

The person I had known briefly on Skype as my father.

AUTHOR'S NOTE

The initial idea for this novel came from a regular Skype meeting with my son who lives in Sydney. I pondered the question 'what if' someone viewed an assault from the other side of the world. The broad plot outline came later, after news reports of increased racist attacks in the aftermath of the Brexit referendum.

I took advantage of my visits to my son when he was working in London to provide background to some of the locations mentioned in this book. Likewise I have drawn on my experiences during my visit to Sydney in the Autumn of 2019, particularly to Government House on the one very wet day of my stay. For the record, the staff there were marvellous, allowing us to bring my baby granddaughter's pushchair into the building out of the rain.

As in two of my previous novels (A Matter of Degree and One Degree Over) I could not resist bringing in a reference to my childhood home town of Shoreham-by Sea.

I had originally intended to make a direct link between the Railway Terraces in Lewisham, London, and Lewisham, Sydney but, as mentioned in the text, I thought it would be just one coincidence too many!

I should like to thank Anne Bendix for her opinions on the intital draft and Mecki Testroet and Jeremy Child for their more detailed proof reading.

Colin Andrews
August 2020

Lightning Source UK Ltd.
Milton Keynes UK
UKHW011948211220
375665UK00002B/71